"Burke. What are you doing here?" Louetta asked.

He stepped into the aisle, his eyes never leaving her face. "I told you I'd be back."

In two months, Louetta thought. That's what he'd said *two and a half years ago.*

"Do you keep your promises?" Burke asked quietly.

In her mind, she saw Burke as he'd been that April night, winded from his trek into town, devastatingly rugged and handsome. She slipped into his hazel eyes that night, fell into the warmth of his rare smiles. Something soft and warm nudged Louetta from inside, something she might have called hope a long, long time ago.

But she knew she had to find the strength to send Burke on his way. After all, she had to run her diner, attend Ladies' Aid Society meetings, organize the annual Christmas pageant. And consider marrying a man she didn't love....

Dear Reader,

Happy Holidays! Our gift to you is all the very best Romance has to offer, starting with *A Kiss, a Kid and a Mistletoe Bride* by RITA-Award winning author Lindsay Longford. In this VIRGIN BRIDES title, when a single dad returns home at Christmas, he encounters the golden girl he'd fallen for one magical night a lifetime ago. Can his kiss—and his kid—win her heart and make her a mistletoe mom?

Rising star Susan Meier continues her TEXAS FAMILY TIES miniseries with *Guess What? We're Married!* And no one is more shocked than the amnesiac bride in this sexy, surprising story! In *The Rich Gal's Rented Groom,* the next sparkling installment of Carolyn Zane's THE BRUBAKER BRIDES, a rugged ranch hand poses as Patsy Brubaker's husband at her ten-year high school reunion. But this gal voted Most Likely To Succeed won't rest till she wins her counterfeit hubby's heart! BUNDLES OF JOY meets BACHELOR GULCH in a fairy-tale romance by beloved author Sandra Steffen. When a shy beauty is about to accept *another* man's proposal, her true-blue *true* love returns to town, bearing *Burke's Christmas Surprise*.

Who wouldn't want to be *Stranded with a Tall, Dark Stranger*— especially an embittered ex-cop in need of a good woman's love? Laura Anthony's tale of transformation is perfect for the holidays! And speaking of transformations... Hayley Gardner weaves an adorable, uplifting tale of a Grinch-like hero who becomes a Santa Claus daddy when he receives *A Baby in His Stocking*.

And in the New Year, look for our fabulous new promotion FAMILY MATTERS and Romance's first-ever six-book continuity series, LOVING THE BOSS, in which office romance leads six friends down the aisle.

Happy Holidays!

Mary-Theresa Hussey
Senior Editor, Silhouette Romance

Please address questions and book requests to:
Silhouette Reader Service
U.S.: 3010 Walden Ave., P.O. Box 1325, Buffalo, NY 14269
Canadian: P.O. Box 609, Fort Erie, Ont. L2A 5X3

Sandra Steffen

BURKE'S CHRISTMAS SURPRISE

Silhouette
R O M A N C E™
Published by Silhouette Books
America's Publisher of Contemporary Romance

For Linda Thelen,
a beautiful writer, trustworthy confidant, talented
critiquer and a great phone buddy.
We haven't actually solved the world's problems, but
we've analyzed most of them.
Merry Christmas.

SILHOUETTE BOOKS

ISBN 0-373-19337-8

BURKE'S CHRISTMAS SURPRISE

Copyright © 1998 by Sandra E. Steffen

This edition published by arrangement with Harlequin Books S.A.

Printed in U.S.A.

SANDRA STEFFEN

Her fans tell Sandra how much they enjoy her fictional characters, especially her male fictional characters. That's not so surprising, because although this award-winning, bestselling author believes every character is a challenge, she has the most fun with the men she creates, whether they're doctors or cowboys, toddlers or teenagers. Perhaps that's because she's surrounded by so many men—her husband, their four sons, her dad, brothers, in-laws. She feels blessed to be surrounded by just as many warm, intelligent and funny women.

Growing up the fourth child of ten in a family of ambitious and opinionated people, she developed a keen appreciation for laughter and argument, for stubborn people with hearts of gold and intelligent people who aren't afraid of other intelligent people. Sandra lives in Michigan with her husband, three of their sons and a blue-eyed mutt who thinks her name is No-Molly-No. Sandra's book, *Child of Her Dreams*, won the 1994 National Readers' Choice Award. Several of her titles have appeared on national bestseller lists.

Dear Reader,

I love books about babies, because when I read about a bundle of joy, I remember mine. I'll never forget the wonder of my first baby, of looking into his eyes, and of smelling that amazing newborn scent. It was love at first sight, but it was terror at first sight, too. Oh my gosh! What did I know about caring for someone so tiny and helpless? My husband and I laughed and cried our way through it, and by the time our first was six, we'd presented him with three little brothers. Although we knew a lot more about parenting by then, the wonder of holding each of them for the first time, of looking into their eyes and of smelling their newborn scents, never diminished. Neither did the fear. Oh my gosh! What did I know about caring for someone so tiny and helpless and one or two or three others?

All my bundles of joy are driving now. One has braces, one has an earring and—gulp—all are dating. It's because of them that my life motto is Never Wait Till The Last Minute To Worry. I've learned that with the worry comes the wonder, for you see, every time I hug them, I'm reminded of how far they've come and where they began. So here's to bundles of joy—those in books, those in our arms and those in our memories.

Sincerely,

Sandra Steffen

Chapter One

Outwardly, not much had changed in Jasper Gulch, South Dakota. But then, it wasn't the outward changes Burke Kincaid was concerned about. He pulled in to the last available parking space on Main Street, pushing his car door open before he'd even cut the engine and lights. Snow flurries stung his face as he made a beeline for the diner across the street. He stopped a foot short of the door, one hand on the handle, the other deep in the pocket of his black overcoat. This was it. The moment of truth. The moment he'd been waiting for for two and a half years.

God. Two and a half years.

His arrival was going to be a surprise. Hell, it was going to be a shock. He'd spent many a sleepless night trying to decide how to handle it. He could have called or written. But what could he have said? "Hi, Lily. This is Burke. Burke Kincaid. I don't know if you remember me or not, but you and I spent one incredibly passionate night together a few years ago, and I was hoping—"

What was he hoping? That she wanted to take up where they'd left off? That she remembered?

He remembered.

Lily's gray eyes had been filled with dreams, her pale skin prone to blushes that night when he'd hiked into town after running out of gas near the village limits. He'd had every intention of simply using her telephone to call for a lift and a gas can, then continuing on his way to Oklahoma City where he'd planned to visit his half brother. But Lily had smiled at him, and he'd lost all sense of direction, all sense, period. He'd followed her into her tiny kitchen where she was brewing a pot of tea. He supposed that first kiss had been inevitable, being near her in such a tight space. The second had thrown him for a loop, but it was nothing compared to how he'd felt when he'd discovered he was her first lover. She had a body a man could lose himself in, lose his mind over. He would have been back sooner. If only...

No. He'd already spent too much time on "if only." He couldn't change the past any more than he could control it. Today was what mattered. Today, and what happened in the next ten minutes.

The bell jingled over the door when he stepped inside the diner. The lights were on, and more than a dozen cowboy hats hung on pegs near the door, but the tables and booths were empty. Following the noise to an open door in the back, Burke entered a room that was nearly bursting with ranchers and cowboys. His gaze immediately searched the handful of women. None was Lily.

A short man with thinning gray hair and intelligent blue eyes rushed over. "Glad you could make it," Doc Masey said, shaking Burke's hand. "Have a good trip?"

"Uneventful," Burke answered, continuing to search the crowd.

"Good, good." The old doctor removed his wire-rimmed glasses and painstakingly cleaned them on a white handkerchief he took from his pocket. Holding them up to the light, he said, "My wife used to insist that if she couldn't see in, I couldn't see out. Wise woman, God rest her soul."

Before Burke could do more than nod, the doctor rushed on. "Isn't usually this much of a hubbub before our town meetings, but tonight our very own rodeo champion is gonna ask one of our local gals to marry him, and a lot of folks have turned out to watch."

Burke's second nod was interrupted by a commotion in the front of the room. A man with a limping cowboy swagger strolled to a podium and called, "Folks, would you take your seats so I can get this show on the road?"

Boots thudded and metal chairs creaked as the men and women of Jasper Gulch moseyed to their places. Taking a seat next to Doc Masey, Burke scanned the crowd. There was a lot of whisker stubble, a lot of flannel and faded denim, a lot of indentations in hair where a cowboy hat normally sat. Five rows up and a dozen seats over, a woman with wavy brown hair turned her head slightly.

Lily.

The noise receded and Burke's thoughts froze. In some far corner of his mind he heard Doc Masey explaining how the town had been dying due to the shortage of women, and how the town council had decided to advertise for women three years ago. The names of some of the *gals* who had answered that ad meant nothing to Burke; *his* attention was trained on a woman who had grown up here.

He'd almost convinced himself that his memories had enhanced Lily's beauty. In reality, his memories hadn't done her justice. Her skin was as pale as he remembered, her hair was slightly shorter, waving to her shoulders instead of halfway down her back. Her smile was serene, regal. How had so much beauty gone undetected all these years? Were these ranchers and cowboys blind?

He wanted to call her name, imagined smiling as he watched recognition settle across her features. Before he could do more than lean ahead in his chair, the man at the front of the room said, "Louetta, come on up here, dar-lin'."

Burke was a little surprised when Lily rose to her feet. By the time she'd wended her way to the front of the room, realization had dawned and any thought he might have had of smiling slid away.

"What's going on?"

"That's Wes Stryker," Doc Masey explained. "He won the national rodeo championship two years running. The last broken bone brought him hobbling home for good. Can't say I blame him. Trophies and awards aren't worth a lick compared to the love of a good woman."

"What does that have to do with Lily?"

"Who?"

Half the crowd shushed the other half. And then Wes Stryker lowered himself stiffly to one knee. Holding his hat over his heart, the former rodeo champion reached for Lily's hand. Through the roaring din in Burke's ears, he heard the other man say, "I know I haven't been around much since we were kids, and I've got more aches and pains than men twice my age, but I'm hardworkin', and I'd be honored if you'd agree to be my wife. What do you say? Will you marry me, Louetta?"

Why was that cowboy calling Lily "Louetta"? Burke swallowed hard and slowly rose to his feet. "That's going to be difficult," he called, his voice carrying over the sudden hubbub as all eyes turned to see who had spoken.

"What did he say?"

"Who is that?"

"What does he mean, it's gonna be difficult?"

Burke's gaze met Lily's, and his voice faded, losing its steely edge. "It's going to be difficult," he repeated, "because you already promised to marry me."

"Did he say what I think he said?" one of the old-timers asked.

"Shh," someone called.

"Shh, yourself."

Louetta Graham recognized the voices of people she'd known all her life, but she couldn't drag her gaze from the man in the back of the room. White shirt, wool pants, windblown hair. *Burke.* With her heart beating against her chest like a sledgehammer on cement, she said, "What are you doing here?"

He stepped sideways into the aisle, his eyes never leaving her face. "I told you I'd be back."

In two months, Louetta thought, one hand going to her neck. That's what he'd said *two and a half years* ago.

"Do you keep your promises?" Burke asked quietly.

Something soft and warm nudged Louetta from inside, something she might have called hope a long, long time ago. Her heart rate quickened, her face grew hot and a traitorous softness drew her attention to the very core of her body. In her mind she saw Burke as he'd been that April night, winded from his trek into town, devastatingly rugged and handsome. She'd slipped into his hazel eyes that night, had fallen into the warmth of his rare smiles. It was happening again. She was losing herself in him, one slow inch at a time.

"What do you say?" Wes Stryker asked, rising stiffly to his feet.

"Yes," Burke said. "What do you say?"

Louetta couldn't believe this was happening. She'd known Wes Stryker was going to ask her to marry him tonight. She'd been rehearsing what she was going to say. He was quite a catch for a woman like her. Everyone thought so. He'd returned to Jasper Gulch a few times each year since joining the rodeo circuit when he was fresh out of school. The last set of broken ribs and the dislocated shoulder and sprained ankle he'd gotten after being bucked off and trampled by an ornery bronco had brought him home for good. At thirty-five, he said he was too old, too tired, too worn for the rodeo circuit. Rumor had it that he was looking for a wholesome woman to grow old with, one who wouldn't run out on him the first time something better came along. Louetta had been as surprised as everyone else when he'd come a-callin' on her. Wes Stryker didn't make her heart chug to life, but she was pretty sure he wouldn't break it, either.

Burke Kincaid had already broken it clean in two.

"Are you gonna marry me?" Wes's voice finally drew her gaze. Tears blurred her vision and thickened her throat as she stared into his blue eyes. "Are you?" he repeated.

"I—I mean—I thought. But now I d-don't—" Since stammering was getting her nowhere, she clamped her mouth shut and shrugged helplessly.

"Are you gonna marry him?" Wes asked.

Her gaze shifted from one man to the other. Burke was watching her. His eyes appeared dark from here, his hair mussed, his features striking and strong. Certain her face was beet red, she shrugged all over again.

"Hot dang, Stryker," Boomer Brown declared from the second row. "It looks like your competin' days ain't over after all."

"That's right," someone else declared.

"Yee-haw! Who said nothin' ever happens in small towns? This has all the makings of a mighty interesting season."

The dazed expression Wes usually wore these days broke for an instant, a smile spreading across his tired features as he faced the Jasper Gents. "I'm beginning to think this might just be exactly what the doctor ordered."

"Well, what do ya know about that," somebody else murmured loud enough for Louetta to hear. "The girl voted most likely not to by her graduating class has two—count 'em—two suitors."

"Oh, my," Louetta whispered, searching frantically for a place to sit down while she still had control of her feet.

"Oh, dear," Isabell Pruitt called in her shrill, nasal voice. "I do believe Louetta is going to faint. Jed, let her have your chair. Hurry."

Louetta sank into the chair and immediately bent over, placing her head between her knees. "There, there," Isabell assured her, patting her arm. "That's it. Take a deep breath. Now another. Oh, I wish your mother were here. She'd have her smelling salts with her. Doc Masey!"

Louetta felt the usual stab of pain at the mention of her mother, but since Isabell missed Opal as much as she did, Louetta tipped her head to one side and said, "I'm pretty sure Mother took her smelling salts with her to heaven. It's all right, Isabell, I think the worst is over."

Louetta's voice sounded distant in her own ears, but her vision was starting to clear and she could feel her heart rate returning to normal. She sat up tentatively, and wavered Isabell a feeble smile.

That's it, Louetta told herself. *You can make it through this without causing a bigger scene.*

Mind reeling, she vowed to hold herself together until the meeting ended. Then she would take the time to have the nervous breakdown she deserved. First, she would have to find the strength to send Burke on his way. Maybe then things would get back to normal. She would run her newly

purchased diner, spend time with her friends, attend Ladies
Aid Society meetings, organize the annual Christmas pageant and consider marrying a man she didn't love.

That's it. Take a deep breath. Now another. As soon as
this meeting was over, she would tell Burke what she
thought of him and his unannounced visit. After that, she
would make her way up to her apartment. She would close
the door, turn out the lights and pull the blankets over her
head.

Luckily, Jasper Gulch town meetings rarely took long.
Luke Carson was calling for order right now. Just as she'd
thought, old business was taken care of in a matter of
minutes. An argument broke out between Bonnie Trumble,
who owned Bonnie's Clip & Curl, and Edith Ferguson,
who thought the town should adopt an ordinance concerning the use of certain colors of paint on the buildings lining
Main Street. "The beauty parlor is neon green!" Edith exclaimed. "Why, it's despicable."

Personally, Louetta liked the new color. It had punch. It
had pizzazz. It had personality. It got a person's attention
without saying a word. As a woman who had been a wallflower her entire life, Louetta liked those qualities, even if
the beauty shop did stick out like a sore thumb. Thankfully,
the issue was tabled until the following month, which
meant that the meeting was nearly over.

"Now," Luke Carson called from the front of the room,
"before we adjourn, Doc Masey has something he'd like
to say. Doc?"

Chairs creaked as folks folded their arms at their chests
and shifted their positions. Louetta stifled a moan, because
as much as she loved the old doctor, the man was notorious
for making a long story unbearable. She hoped he decided
to make an exception tonight. Taking his white handkerchief from his pocket, he began polishing his wire-rimmed

spectacles. When he started in about how he'd been a doctor in this town for nigh on fifty years, Louetta closed her eyes and sighed.

Before he'd gotten halfway into his tale of how he'd brought Neil Anderson into the world during a blizzard in '58, Cletus McCully interrupted. "Doc, I swear you could talk the ears off a deaf man. I ain't necessarily gonna live forever, ya know. Would you get to the point?"

Another time Louetta might have smiled, but she glanced over her shoulder, straight into Burke's eyes, and she couldn't have smiled if her life had depended upon it.

"Burke," Doc called. "Come on up here, would ya?"

What could Burke possibly have to do with Doc Masey?

Like the quiet before the storm, silence filled the room. Surely Louetta's heart wasn't the only one thumping a little wildly at the way Burke carried himself, at the width of his shoulders, the fit of his black pants. However, it was highly likely that she was the only woman who averted her eyes.

"As you all know," Doc Masey declared, "I've been searching for a replacement for a few years now. I'm pleased to say I've found one. Looks like he got the jump on me, but I like a man who knows his own mind. Folks, I'd like you to meet my new partner, Dr. Burke Kincaid."

Louetta's head came up, her heart rising to her throat. "What did Doc say?" she asked Lisa McCully, the young woman sitting next to her.

"It looks like Doc Masey's taken on one of your fiancés as a new partner," Lisa whispered.

"One of my—"

A freight train sounded in Louetta's ears. The lights went dim, her muscles turned to liquid. And she keeled over in a deep faint.

* * *

Louetta came to amid a blur of faces and a whir of voices.

"She fainted, you say?"

"Is she gonna be all right?"

"How would I know? I ain't no doctor."

"There's no need to snap my head off."

"Boys, would you give me a little room?"

Louetta recognized Doc Masey's voice. Although she couldn't quite make out the two cowboys who were stepping out of the way, she could see Isabell hovering over her right shoulder, Doc Masey over her left. Burke's and Wes's faces were inches apart, and someone—a quick glance at the masculine hand touching her wrist told her it was Burke—was taking her pulse.

"Are you all right?" His voice was edged in velvet, just as it had been that night two and a half years ago.

"Of course she's all right. You are all right, aren't you?" Wes asked.

Louetta nodded and tried to sit up. Had she really fainted before a roomful of people? Lord, her humiliation was nearly complete.

"I'm fine. I'd really like to go up to my apartment now."

Suddenly Burke was bending down, gliding his arms underneath her, lifting her up. No, she thought, her dark purple skirt hitched up around her thighs, her white sweater askew, her face inches away from his, *now* her humiliation was complete.

"Please," she protested, "I can walk."

"For heaven's sake," Isabell sputtered, "put her down this instant. Haven't you done enough?"

Burke eyed the old biddy over the top of Louetta's head. As far as he was concerned, he hadn't done nearly enough. He hadn't kissed Lily or Louetta or whatever the hell her name was. He hadn't explained. He had yet to see her smile.

Wes Stryker's voice cut into Burke's thoughts. "She said she can walk."

Reading the challenge in Stryker's eyes, Burke tightened his grip around Louetta. Wes took a step closer and held Burke's stare.

"Come on, you two," insisted a woman with large brown eyes, a sultry voice and a protruding stomach that indicated a baby was due in a month or two. "Why don't you go shoot some bottles off a fence or duke it out over at the Crazy Horse or do whatever else men do to compete for a woman's hand. Melody, Jillian and I can take it from here. That okay with you, Louetta?"

As a doctor, Burke supposed the blush on Lily's cheeks was a good sign. As a man, he didn't want to let her out of his arms, let alone out of his sight. Since she nodded at the pregnant woman, he didn't see what choice he had. He lowered her feet to the floor, slowly stepping aside as two women each slid an arm around Lily's back.

There was a lot of noise all around him as people spoke amongst themselves. Burke stayed where he was, watching Lily walk away, regal even now.

He'd imagined her reaction to his return a hundred times. He would have liked her to welcome him with open arms. He would have settled for a small smile and a shy hello. He supposed he should have known this wasn't going to be easy. Nothing about the past two and a half years had been easy.

She stopped suddenly in the doorway and glanced over her shoulder, bravely meeting his eyes. Her lips trembled. Although she didn't smile, a look passed between them. He swallowed, but it only made him aware of the pulsing sensation in his throat and the growing pressure much lower.

Burke could feel all eyes on him, and he knew that this wasn't the time or the place to say what he'd come here to say. Meeting her serious expression with a serious expression of his own, he said, "We'll talk later."

Her throat convulsed on a swallow. Neither nodding nor shaking her head, she allowed the other women to lead her away.

"For a doctor, you have lousy timing."

Burke glanced at the man who had spoken. Wes Stryker looked the way a person would expect an ex-rodeo champion to look, all cheekbones and squint lines and stiff joints, rugged and haggard at the same time. Burke wondered if Lily was in love with the man. While he was at it, he wondered if it was possible that she was still in love with *him*. Releasing a breath he hadn't known he'd been holding, Burke squared off opposite the other man. "Maybe, but I'm told I have a good bedside manner."

Stryker's eyes narrowed. "I'm more concerned about your in-bed manner."

"Sorry. I don't kiss and tell."

The other man's eyebrows rose slightly, and Burke sensed a grudging respect in Wes Stryker's expression.

"You gonna step aside, Wes," somebody called from behind, "and let the new doctor run roughshod over you?"

Wes shook his head. "It looks like Boomer was right. My competin' days aren't over after all."

Burke accepted the challenge, along with the hand Wes held out to him. Wes's knuckles were bony, his palm callused, his grip bordering on painful. Squaring his jaw, Burke squeezed the other man's hand in return.

Wes grunted. "May the best man win."

Burke nodded stiffly, tightening his own grip. "Believe me," he said, wondering whose bones would crack first, "I intend to."

Bets were made among the other men. The old biddy who'd helped Lily earlier insisted that this was exactly the kind of thing the Ladies Aid Society had been afraid would happen. A few old-timers grumbled that folks needed a little fun and excitement now and then, and the meeting was finally adjourned. Burke and Wes might have gone on shaking hands all night if Doc Masey and another old man with white whiskers and tattered suspenders hadn't broken them up.

The man on the right snapped one suspender and rocked back on the heels of worn cowboy boots. "Name's Cletus McCully. Looks like you and Wes are evenly matched. That's gonna make things more interesting, that's for sure. Tell us, boy, where are you from?"

Refusing to give in to the impulse to cradle his right hand in his left one, Burke met the old codger's inquisitive stare. "I grew up in northern Washington. My practice was in Seattle."

"Ah, you must have met our Louetta when she went with her mother to that cancer research hospital last year. Didn't do much good. Opal died right on schedule. She raised Louetta by herself, you know."

No, Burke hadn't known. And that wasn't where he'd met *Louetta*. Since Cletus McCully didn't need to know that, Burke held the old man's piercing stare a few seconds longer, then strode out to the sidewalk with the country doctor.

The snowflakes were getting bigger, the air colder. Several men jaywalked across the street and disappeared inside what appeared to be the town's only bar. Burke glanced up at the lighted window in the small apartment over the diner.

Following the course of Burke's gaze, Doc Masey said, "Looks like you have more reasons than one for taking this job."

Burke nodded, but didn't elaborate.

The ensuing silence didn't deter Doc Masey in the least. "No matter what the boys say, I don't like the looks of this. It has trouble written all over it. Two men. One woman. Nope. Don't like the looks of it one bit."

"She's not just any woman," Burke said quietly.

"You love her."

It was a statement, not a question, but Burke found himself nodding anyway. "Until I met her, I didn't know I was capable. But yes, I love her. I have since the day I met her."

"There'll be hell to pay if you hurt her."

Inhaling a deep breath of cold November air, Burke could hardly blame the old doctor for the warning. Miles Masey wasn't stupid. Everyone had seen how Lily had reacted to Burke's arrival. A person didn't faint for no reason. Although they obviously didn't know the circumstances, Burke had already hurt her. Oh, he'd had good reasons. The question was, would she be able to forgive him?

Tucking his chin inside the collar of his black overcoat, he accepted the key from Doc Masey's outstretched hand and turned down the old man's offer to escort him to his new residence. He was perfectly capable of getting settled into his new place by himself. Once he was settled, he would find Lily, or Louetta, or whatever folks around here called her. And he would try to explain.

Chapter Two

"**W**ere those footsteps I heard on the stairs?"

Louetta pushed the cool cloth off her forehead and swung her feet over the side of her flowered sofa. Sitting up, she pretended not to notice the looks Lisa McCully and Melody and Jillian Carson cast one another.

"I didn't hear a thing," Melody said, taking her turn checking the stairs.

"Me, neither," Lisa agreed, trying to find a comfortable position on the rocking chair across the room.

Jillian simply smiled encouragingly at Louetta, who dropped her face into her hands in defeat. In her defense, there *had* been footsteps on the stairs when Isabell, Doc Masey and a few of the members of the Ladies Aid Society had come up to check on her. The last visitor had left more than an hour ago, and Louetta was beginning to worry she was hearing things.

"Goodness gracious, I'm a wreck. Worse, I'm probably the talk of the town."

"Everyone's the talk of Jasper Gulch," Melody said,

toying with a strand of shoulder-length blond hair as she dropped onto a cushion on the floor. "Folks still talk about the time I dressed up in platform shoes, a skirt up to here and a shirt down to there to teach Clayt a lesson."

Brown eyes flashing, Lisa declared, "And after word got out that Wyatt and I were trying to have a baby, folks stopped me on the street to ask if I was pregnant yet. You wouldn't believe some of the advice I got. Why, Mertyl Gentry, of all people, told me to try standing on my head in a corner, after, well, you get the picture."

Jillian Carson brushed her wispy red hair off her forehead and leaned ahead in her chair. "Is that how junior here came about?"

Laughing, Lisa said, "Junior here came to be because of her daddy's philosophy. 'If at first you don't succeed, try, try again.'"

Even Louetta forgot about her discomfiture long enough to laugh at that one. Some people took friendships for granted. Not her. Until Jillian and Lisa had moved to Jasper Gulch, Louetta's only friends had been the members of the Ladies Aid Society, women who were closer to her mother's age than hers. Although Melody had been three or four years behind Louetta in school, she was one of the few people in town who had always made it a point to give Louetta more than a nod in passing. Still, they hadn't become good friends until a few years ago when Louetta had gotten up her courage and had taken that first painful step out of her shell.

Lisa, Melody and Jillian had all brought laughter into Louetta's life, but Melody was the one Louetta felt closest to. The two of them had grown up right here in a town chock-full of rugged cowboys and ranchers. And the two of them had been overlooked by each and every one of those cowboys and ranchers for years. Melody had finally snagged the man she'd been in love with all her life. Now she and Clayt Carson had eleven-year-old Haley, and two little boys, twenty-two-month-old Jordan and newborn Slade.

When Louetta had first decided it was up to *her* to fill the lonely gaps in her own life, she'd been convinced that a few wonderful friends was the most she could hope for. It was certainly more than she'd dreamed she'd have. And then Burke had driven into town. She'd heard stories and whispers about a kind of magic that could sweep a woman right off her feet when the right man came along. Burke had swept into her apartment to use her phone. To this day she couldn't remember how she'd gone from fixing a pot of tea to helping him out of his clothes. Lord, she still blushed when she thought of how totally out of character her behavior had been.

There hadn't been a doubt in her mind that she'd fallen in love. At the time, she'd thought he'd felt the same....

"Earth to Louetta."

"She's either thinking about a man or—"

"Sex. She's thinking about sex."

Once Louetta's vision cleared, the expressions on her friends' faces were enough to send a blush to her cheeks. Melody, Jillian and Lisa were a godsend. No doubt about that. At the moment they were all far too perceptive for her peace of mind.

"Were those footsteps I heard on the stairs?" Louetta asked again, straining to hear.

After Lisa had taken her turn checking, Louetta said, "I'm really sorry about this. And I appreciate everything the three of you have done. I'm fine now, and I think you should go home to your husbands and—" she looked at Melody and Jillian "—your children."

After ten minutes' worth of reassurances from Louetta

that she was really and truly over her fainting spell, the other three women finally left. Alone, Louetta wandered through the tiny apartment she'd been living in these past three years. Tilting the blinds, she peered down at Main Street. A handful of cars were parked in front of the Crazy Horse Saloon across the street, but not a soul was in sight.

Although the time of year had been different, the street had looked this way that night two and a half years ago, too. Arms folded at her waist, Louetta had been looking out the window when she'd noticed a man walking down the middle of the street. His gait was different from that of the ranchers and cowboys who lived around here. And yet, as she'd opened the window and leaned out, fear hadn't crossed her mind.

"Can I help you?" she'd called.

He'd stopped and glanced around, slowly raising his head. Dressed in dark clothes, a long black coat and city shoes, his tall, broad-shouldered frame had cast a herculean shadow.

"I seem to have run out of gas near the village limits," he'd said, the wind ruffling through his dark hair.

Something must have been in the air, or in his eyes, because suddenly Louetta had felt like Rapunzel or some other beautiful fairy-tale princess. "I don't own a car, but I could go back to the wedding reception being held in the town hall and ask one of the local men to give you a lift and a can of gas if you're sure that's what's wrong."

He'd shrugged sheepishly, and had taken a few steps closer. Lowering his voice as if revealing a secret, he'd said, "I know men are supposed to be mechanically inclined, but I really hate engines. Could you just point me in the direction of the nearest gas station?"

Butterflies had fluttered in Louetta's stomach. Not just a few, but an entire flock of them. It made her bold and daring and giddy. "Nothing's open this time of night," she'd answered. "But you can use my phone if you want to call a wrecker in Pierre."

She'd directed him around to the back, and she'd let him in, taking the steps to her apartment ahead of him. She'd expected there to be long, tension-filled stretches of silence. After all, she was Louetta Graham, the shiest woman on the planet. But the smile he'd slanted her way had broken through her horrible timidness, and the butterflies in her stomach had moved over to make room for another sensation entirely. Some people would have called it attraction. She'd called it magic.

It had to be magic. It was the only explanation she'd been able to come up with for the way she'd been able to talk to him, and laugh with him, and make love with him. She'd fallen in love that night. There was no doubt about that. Her doubts had come later, when he'd failed to return.

She'd believed him when he'd promised to come back as soon as he'd taken care of business back home. "Two months, no more," he'd whispered huskily, lingering over his goodbye kiss.

Ah, yes, she'd believed him, heart and soul. She'd waited patiently those two months, but as the days had turned into weeks, and the weeks into months, her heart had broken and her dreams had been lost.

She'd been naive for a thirty-three-year-old woman, and yet, after that one night with Burke, she'd never felt more like a woman in her life. A searing loneliness stabbed at her. She hadn't felt that way again in all the time he'd been gone.

Staring at the lighted window of the Crazy Horse Saloon across the street, Louetta knew that seeing Burke again was what had brought so many dark emotions back to the surface. She hadn't been able to help the tiny flicker of hope that had sprung to life when he'd said they would talk later. That had been three hours ago. He wasn't going to come. When would she learn?

She *had* learned, she told herself. She wasn't the same woman she'd been two and a half years ago. Thank heavens. Day by day, she'd replaced her quiet hopelessness with determination. Bit by bit, she'd realized she liked the new Louetta Graham. She might always be shy, but she was less introverted. And she'd finally struck out on her own. She'd purchased the diner and her apartment. She was slowly becoming an active member of the community. She had friends and she had goals. Some were far-reaching. Others pertained to today.

No more blushing every time she remembered how it had felt to be in Burke's arms.

No more reliving every detail of the night they'd met.

No more silly daydreams about what might have been.

No more waiting on pins and needles and listening for footsteps on the stairs.

"Hello, Lily."

She spun around, the hand that had flown to her throat slowly falling to her side. Burke stood in her doorway, the light in the hallway throwing his shadow into the room. She closed her eyes. When he was still there when she opened them again, she willed her heart to settle back into its rightful place. Darn him for unraveling so many of her vows in the blink of an eye. Darn him, darn him, darn him.

"May I come in?"

She found herself nodding, but she couldn't force any words past the knot in her throat.

"The place looks good," he said, folding his overcoat over the back of a chair. "Different. It suits you better now."

Darn him, darn him, darn him for saying the one thing

in all the world that could soften her resolve. She'd been living in this apartment for three years, but she'd purchased it only a year ago, after Melody had learned that she and Clayt were expecting a second child close on the heels of their first. Louetta had welcomed the opportunity to buy the diner, using the money her dear mother had left her after she'd died. At first, painting and wallpapering had been something to do to fill Louetta's time now that her mother was gone. Nobody had been more surprised than Louetta when she'd discovered she had a flair for decorating. And nobody was more proud of their home.

"How are you feeling?"

He was probably referring to her fainting episode, but at the moment she didn't care. "Fine, and you? I mean, you look pretty good for somebody who just woke up from a coma or was released from prison in some third-world country."

He nodded stiffly. "I deserved that. I thought about calling. Writing. I'm afraid it's easier to ask for forgiveness than for permission."

Louetta held very still, grappling with her conscience. Asking him to sit down would have been the polite thing to do. The old Louetta had been nothing if not polite. Folding the afghan Lisa had used earlier, Louetta reminded herself that the old Louetta was gone. Thank God. And although few people could put their finger on exactly what had changed, *she* was aware of the differences.

"Yes, well, the easy way isn't always the right way," she said stoically.

He'd strolled to the other side of the room, where a shelf held several photographs. He turned slowly, and she couldn't help noticing how easily he moved. There was an air of efficiency about him. It was there in the way he shortened the distance between them, in the way he spoke, in the way he looked at her.

"No matter what you think, I didn't take the easy way out two years ago." He started to continue, stopped and tried again. "I know this is awkward," he said quietly.

She nodded again. Strangely, there hadn't been any awkwardness between them the first time they'd met. Of course, two and a half years of soul-searching, of waiting and hoping and not knowing hadn't been between them then.

"What are you doing here, Burke?"

Burke opened his mouth to speak, but his gaze flicked over her, and he forgot what he was going to say. She'd been wearing a simple cotton dress, prim and proper in every way, the first time they'd met. Although the skirt and sweater she was wearing tonight weren't blatantly sexy, they fit her body perfectly, accentuating instead of hiding. "You're as pretty as a picture."

For a moment he thought she was going to smile. Instead, she tucked a wavy strand of hair behind her ear and made a disparaging sound. "You and Wes could both use a lesson in originality."

For a moment, Burke's brow furrowed. But then he noticed the poinsettia plant sitting on the low table in front of him, and understanding dawned. "Stryker's already sent you flowers?"

She shrugged. "It has all the markings of the Crazy Horse crowd."

"Mind if I read the card?"

"Be my guest."

It took Burke longer to reach for the card than it did to read the poem written in a man's messy scrawl. "Roses are red, violets are like paint. I got you these flowers, but a poet I ain't."

Burke made a derisive sound. "You're considering marrying a man who writes poetry like that?"

Louetta's head came up, vexation flashing in her eyes. "Wes is a rodeo rider, not a writer."

Shaking his head, Burke couldn't help remembering the summer his stepbrother had spent reciting "There Once Was a Man from Oklahoma." Glancing at the card, he said, "I suppose it contains a certain sincerity."

"Wes Stryker is very sincere."

Burke didn't like the direction this conversation was taking. He'd come here to try to explain. The last thing he wanted to talk about was Lily's relationship with another man.

But Lily was pacing on the other side of the room, talking as she went. "Wes was one of the few people who didn't tease the living daylights out of me when we were kids. He always had an easygoing smile and a kind disposition."

"How long have you and Stryker been an item?"

"I've been seeing him for several weeks now."

"Do you love him?" Burke caught a whiff of her perfume, and the question he wanted to ask—*Do you love me?*—went unsaid.

"That's none of your business, Burke."

He was across the room in a flash, the coffee table with its scraggly red plant and hand-written card the only thing separating them. "Maybe not," he said, his voice deceptively low. "That doesn't mean I'm not curious. Have you ever awakened him in the middle of the night with a whisper and a strategically placed kiss?"

Everything inside Louetta went perfectly still. Her cheeks were probably flaming. For once, she didn't care. Darn him for reminding her of how wanton she'd been that night. Darn him for stretching her emotions tighter with every passing second. Darn him for making her aware of a warming sensation low in her belly. Darn him, darn him, darn him.

"This may come as a surprise to you," she said, turning her back to Burke as she stared unseeing out the window. "But I don't hop into bed with every man who leaves a five-dollar tip."

"I never said you did, dammit."

She turned slowly, her skirt swishing around her knees, a lock of hair falling onto her forehead. There was a quiver in her fingertips as she smoothed the tresses out of her eyes. She's changed, Burke thought. Her voice was as soft as always, her eyes the same gray he remembered. The blame in them, however, was brand-new.

He'd hurt her. And she'd found him guilty without hearing his explanation, his reasons. He didn't really blame her. Two and a half years *was* a long time. No one knew that better than he did.

There was no excuse for the need running through him, no excuse for the determination to change her mind. No excuse except he wanted her. No matter what she thought, what had happened between them hadn't been all his doing. Two and a half years ago she'd changed his plans for the evening with one heart-stopping smile. There wasn't much he wouldn't do to see her smile at him like that again.

"Would you tell me something?" he asked.

It probably took a lot of courage to meet his gaze the way she did. It required a lot of strength on his part to keep his feet planted where they were. "Would you have said yes to Stryker's proposal if I hadn't shown up tonight?"

Her shoulders stiffened, her back straightened. "To tell you the truth, I wasn't a hundred percent sure, but I was thinking about telling Wes 'maybe.' He would have made a joke out of that in front of everyone. He's very patient, and very funny.'' She stopped, gazing into the distance. "And very honest. I don't believe *he's* ever told a real lie.''

Burke felt something he didn't much like uncoil deep inside him. Jealousy, anger and finally, grim acceptance. "Sounds like a hell of a guy," he declared. *"Lily."*

Reaching for his coat, he turned on his heel.

The door closed just short of a slam, Burke's footsteps on the stairs echoing through Louetta's small apartment. Lowering her hands from her cheeks, she stared at the door, wondering how she could have failed to hear the thud of footsteps when Burke had arrived.

Up until the moment he'd uttered that last word, she'd thought the meeting was going quite well, all things considered. The conversation may have been a little stilted, but at least she'd kept from blurting out how she'd waited for him during those first months when she'd believed he would return, how she'd died a little more inside with every passing week. She'd kept her feelings inside, remaining strong throughout the entire conversation.

And then he'd gone and called her Lily.

Her feet carried her to the window as if they had a mind of their own. She didn't want to watch Burke walk away, but she couldn't help herself. She remembered how he'd looked up at her from the middle of the street that long-ago April night. Tonight he used the sidewalk, his strides long and powerful. He'd put on his coat, but he hadn't bothered to button it, the wind billowing the dark fabric behind him. Tonight he didn't look back.

"Lily," she'd whispered the night they'd met. *"My name is Lily Graham."*

He'd shaken her hand, his smile one of wonder, his touch simple, natural, undemanding and just firm enough to let her know he was glad to be with her. Simple or not, it had started a fire in her, and had caused her to do and say things she'd never done and said before.

She would never forget how deep his voice had dipped when he'd told her the name suited her. She would never forget how it had sounded when he'd murmured it in the dark of night and in the wee hours of the morning.

Lily hadn't been a painfully shy woman who'd been voted "the girl most likely not to" by the boys in her graduating class. They'd thought it was funny, but it had hurt, just as a thousand other small things had hurt. Her shyness had been a handicap most of her life, one that Louetta had learned to endure, just as she'd learned to hold her head high. *Lily* had been all woman, sure of herself and her rightful place in the universe.

Oh, Burke. Why did you have to come back and remind me of everything I've been missing all these years?

"*Lily,*" Burke had said tonight.

She lowered her head in shame, and wished with all her heart that she was half the woman Lily had been.

One second the cup was in Louetta's hand, the next second it shattered on the floor. She saw it happening, yet she still jumped a mile.

"Slippery little buggers, aren't they?" red-haired Jason Tucker, a twenty-three-year-old ranch hand who could blush as darkly as Louetta, said with a boyish grin.

Nodding, she scooted down to her haunches to pick up the pieces of the second item she'd broken that morning. She was a wreck, that was all there was to it. At this rate, she was going to need another set of dishes by suppertime.

Jed Harley had been very understanding about the milk she'd spilled in his lap, and Boomer Brown hadn't said anything when he'd gotten a saucer full of coffee along with his refill, although his wife, DoraLee, the owner of the Crazy Horse Saloon and Louetta's least likely friend, studied Louetta's face and cast her an understanding smile. Cletus McCully ate without complaining about the eggs she'd scorched, although he did mention that she was as jumpy as a cat on hot bricks.

He was right. She nearly sprang straight into the air every time the bell jangled over the door.

She had no doubt that every one of the usual breakfast crowd noticed her skittishness. They probably attributed it to nerves at the thought of shy little Louetta Graham having two suitors. They had no way of knowing about the guilt sitting like a rock in the middle of her swirling stomach.

Leaving the diners to sip their coffee and mull over their gossip, she used extra care busing the rest of the tables. She felt a headache coming on as she carried the tub of dishes into the kitchen and promptly turned on the tap.

"Girl, ya got a minute?"

"Cletus!" Louetta nearly came out of her skin, the dishes in her hand splashing as she dropped them into the water. "Yes, yes, of course. What is it?"

The old man snapped his suspenders and did such a poor job of pretending to be interested in the fifty-year-old oven that Louetta would have smiled if she'd been physically able.

Choosing a different tack, he shook his craggy old head and glanced at the door. "I'm hiding from those...those manhandlers."

Dropping the clean forks and knives she'd just washed into the rinse water, Louetta heaved a big sigh, but at least she could manage a semblance of a smile. "Are Gussie and Addie Cunningham putting the moves on you again, Cletus?"

"The moves! Jumpin' catfish, those two women are

more wily than sailors and just as determined. What's worse, they don't know the meaning of the word *no*."

Louetta lowered a stack of plates into the deep, stainless steel sink. Gussie Cunningham and her sister Addie had moved to town a couple of years ago, not long after they won the lottery in Wisconsin where they used to live. They were both eccentric, without a doubt. Slightly over sixty and still single, they claimed they were just good old gals who were looking for decent men to call their own.

Up to her elbows in soapsuds, Louetta said, "They're lonely, Cletus. Neither of them means any harm."

"Yeah? Well, I don't mean them any harm, either, but sometimes desperate situations call for desperate measures. And if you don't mind, I think I'll hide out in here for a while. I used to help Melody out now and again, you know. When she had to run an errand, or step out for a minute, I mean, or do something about whatever was causing her to lose sleep at night."

Louetta stopped. Staring past the lines in Cletus's face, into knowing brown eyes, she said, "What makes you think there's someplace else I want to go?"

"Isn't there?"

There was no use wondering how the man could have known. Cletus McCully wasn't much taller than Louetta's five feet seven inches. And yet he was a very big man. Swallowing the lump that came out of nowhere, Louetta closed her eyes and called for courage. Opening them again, she reached behind her back and untied her apron. She handed it to Cletus, and at the last minute kissed his lined cheek. "I know where Melody got her heart."

"Don't go gettin' maudlin on me, girl. And if you slip out the back, nobody has to know you're gone."

Louetta dried her hands on a towel, slipped her coat from the peg by the door. Before she lost her nerve, she stepped into the back alley and headed for a certain doctor's office on Custer Street.

Burke was wandering. Pacing was more like it. The furnished apartment attached to the doctor's office was part of the deal he'd worked out with Doc Masey before agreeing to move to Jasper Gulch. It wasn't the rain that had made his decision to leave Seattle so easy. He'd been feeling dissatisfied, at loose ends, unconnected to his life there for a long time. A thirty-five-year-old doctor in a prestigious city hospital, he'd felt more like a paper shuffler than a physician. Ever since he'd been stranded in this quaint, one-horse town, the idea of treating the same patients for years on end, of making house calls and delivering babies who would grow up and bring *their* babies to him had become a fantasy. Of course, in his fantasy Lily had welcomed him back with open arms.

There was no woman named Lily. She'd been a daydream, a myth. Louetta was real. And Louetta was a lot more stubborn than he'd expected. Hell, she acted as if his soul was darkened by sins, stained by mistakes.

Oh, he'd made his share of mistakes in his life, there was no doubt about that. He wondered what measure God used to gauge a person's wrongs. Was a sin a sin? Or did good intentions balance difficult decisions? Because he'd had the best of intentions. Look where they'd gotten him.

Once he'd arrived back in Seattle two and a half years ago, and he'd faced the fact that he couldn't return to Jasper Gulch, he'd done everything he could to put thoughts of Lily out of his mind. They'd returned when he'd least expected them, unbidden, real enough to touch.

Hell, it was happening right now. He was thirty-five years old. Way too old to be paralyzed by sexual impulses in the middle of the morning. Pacing to the desk, he yanked on the lid of a box filled with books and immediately began placing them on a high shelf. A knock sounded on the door behind him. Continuing his task, he called, "Come on in, Doc. The door's open."

The doorknob jiggled, and the door creaked open.

"Back from your house call so soon?" Burke called without looking.

The room, all at once, was very quiet. Turning, he found Lily standing in the open doorway, the light of a gray November morning behind her, the purse in her hands clutched so tightly her knuckles were white.

"Come in," he said, his voice a low rumble in the still room.

She wet her lips nervously. "I can't stay. I wanted you to know that my name *is* Louetta. But my father always called me Lily."

During the time they'd been apart, Burke had remembered everything about Lily with a clarity that had surprised him. He saw inside her with that same clarity right now. She was scared. Why shouldn't she be? He'd hurt her. The fact that he couldn't have lived with himself if he'd chosen any other way didn't matter. He'd hurt her, and she was none too sure he wouldn't hurt her again.

"I should have known you wouldn't lie," he said, placing a medical book back in the cardboard box.

Her lips parted and she blinked. God, he loved disconcerting her, loved the heat in her eyes and the blush on her cheeks. Something powerful took hold inside him, something elemental, earthy and a lot more pleasant than his earlier frustration. With one hand on his hip and the other in his pocket, he took a step toward her.

The backward step Louetta took was automatic. Good grief. She'd said what she'd come here to say. Now what?

"Well. Er. Um." She nearly groaned out loud. What in

tarnation had happened to her good sense? "I should be going."

"So soon?"

The fact that Burke was steadily moving closer wasn't helping her equilibrium. As one moment stretched to two, she grasped the first excuse that popped into her head. "Isabell usually stops in at the diner about this time of the morning. She's been lonely since Mother died, and she'll worry if I'm not there."

"Does Isabell know about us, *Louetta?*" he said as if trying the name out on his tongue.

Louetta was accustomed to the ever-changing sounds of the breezes that blew here in South Dakota, but she doubted she'd ever be able to hear the sound of the wind after midnight again without being reminded of Burke. His voice was like that wind, a deep sigh, a gentle moaning, a slow sweep across her senses.

"Does she?" he asked again, more quietly than before.

Although it required a conscious effort to pull herself together, she straightened her back and raised her chin a fraction of an inch. Meeting Burke's steady gaze, she said, "Don't worry, Burke. I didn't broadcast our little tryst."

"Is that how you would describe what happened between us? As a tryst?"

A dozen possibilities scrambled through her mind, confusing her even more. "How would you describe it?" she asked.

There was an inherent determination in the set of his chin and a hungry light in his eyes as he said, "It was a damn sight more than that."

His arms were around her before she could take another backward step, and she knew, even before his lips covered hers, that he was going to kiss her.

Chapter Three

Burke moved so fast Louetta's breath caught, her lips parting on a gasp that turned into a sigh the instant his lips covered hers. His arms were strong, the body beneath his charcoal gray sweater warm and solid. She must have closed her eyes, because she couldn't see a thing. But she could feel, and Burke's lips were wet, his chest broad, his heartbeat strong beneath her palm that had somehow come to be pressed between their bodies.

Everything inside her started to swirl together in a slow, heavy spiral, all her thoughts turned to oblivion, all her needs became one. The same thing had happened the first time they'd met. One kiss and she'd been lost, one embrace and she'd craved more. At the time, she hadn't even known what she was craving. Now she knew. And knowing made her need greater and her heart feel more tender at the same time.

She hadn't been aware that they were moving until she felt the cool wall at her back. And then Burke's hands were sliding down her spine, her sweater bunching in his fingers as he pressed her ever closer. His response was unmistakable, her groan of pleasure insuppressible, erupting on a gasp and a sigh.

Need pounded through Burke, dangerous, powerful. He was holding on to Lily tight, with everything he had, and he was still coming apart at the seams. Lord, she was sweet, her breath hot, her hands insistent. And her body, well, it was almost beyond description, her breasts so full and soft, her legs so long, her lips so eager. Her hands spread wide over the fabric of his dress slacks, down the backs of his thighs, and back up again. Desire seared a path from one end of his body to another, making his heart race and all but explode.

He knew he had to stop. He was trying to stop. He never wanted to stop.

Some force had him tangling his fingers in her hair, sending her hair clip tumbling to the floor. The same force had him pulling her hard against him, trying to bury himself in the softness of her body. "Oh, Lily, I've missed you."

The moment those words registered on Louetta's dizzied senses, her eyes opened, and she tensed. She wasn't certain what brought reality crashing all around her—the fact that Burke had called her Lily, or the reminder that there had been two and a half years between them. Two and a half *years* of wondering, of thinking the worst and wishing for a miracle.

As if sensing her disquietude, he took a shuddering breath. She pulled away a little more, and he let her. She made her escape, deftly sidestepping out of his arms and hurrying across the room. "I have to go."

"Stay."

"I can't."

"Lily." And then quieter, more unsure. "Louetta.

Wait." He stopped a few feet away, as if uncertain how close he dared to trod. "I'm glad you came by."

Averting her gaze, she said, "I wanted a clear conscience. I didn't intend..." Her voice trailed away. Honest to Pete, if she blushed, she swore she would walk out the door and not stop until she'd reached the state line.

"I'm glad about that, too," he said quietly.

Her gaze flew to his, and a zing went through her. It happened every time she looked at him, temporal temptation written all over his face. Burke claimed he was glad to see her, glad to have held her. He claimed he'd missed her. Maybe he had. That didn't erase all the pain and loneliness she'd lived with since the night she'd spent with him. He'd had no business kissing her this morning. And she'd had no business responding, not if she wanted to keep the tenacious hold on her pride, not to mention on her heart. Okay. She couldn't change what had happened. He'd kissed her, and she'd let him, for the plain and simple reason that it had felt good. That didn't mean she had to turn all poetic and imagine that she'd found heaven in his arms. There was nothing heavenly or poetic about pain, disillusionment and a broken heart.

"Have dinner with me tonight."

She supposed there was a little consolation in the fact that his voice sounded as shaky as she felt. "I can't."

He reached down and in one lithe movement scooped her purse and the plain ivory barrette off the floor where she hadn't even realized they had fallen. Handing them to her, he said, "You can't?"

She tucked the purse underneath her arm and took the clip into her palm. "I have plans."

"Plans."

She nodded.

There was an edge to his voice when he said, "Could you be a little more specific?"

"I have a date."

"With Stryker?"

"With Wes. Yes."

"You're going out with him after the way you just kissed me?"

Louetta started to shift away from the heavy hint of reproach in his voice, but she caught herself. Bristling, she declared, "I didn't kiss you. *You* kissed *me*." With a flip of her hair over her shoulder and a swing of her hips, she turned around and strode straight out of his house.

Burke watched her from the door, cold wind blowing through his clothes. "Where are you going?" he called to her back.

She spun around so fast her wavy hair twirled into her face. "Back to the diner."

"I mean tonight. With Stryker."

He could see her trying to make sense of the question. She pushed her hair away from her face, pulled the lapels of her coat together and shifted her weight to one foot. Eyebrows raised suspiciously, she said, "We're going to a steak house in Pierre. Why?"

Burke held up both hands innocently. "No reason."

With a roll of her eyes and a shake of her head, she stalked away. He stayed where he was, watching. The woman had a walk that could stop traffic. She also had a temper. She has changed, he thought. Even more surprising—he liked it.

He waited to close the door until she was out of sight. Although the sun wasn't shining, the room seemed brighter somehow, the air more fragrant. There was no doubt about it; the day had just gotten better. He didn't appreciate the fact that Lily was seeing Stryker tonight, but no matter what she said about who'd kissed whom, her response had been an encouraging step in the right direction.

He was a patient man. A doctor couldn't survive without it. Hell, he couldn't have survived his family without patience. Louetta had a date with Stryker tonight. Well, well, well. It was up to Burke to make sure her mind was on the right man. Humming under his breath, he opened the directory and picked up the phone.

Louetta made it back to the diner in record time. She hung up her coat with one hand and reached for a clean apron with the other. Glancing at the stack of clean dishes Cletus was in the process of drying, she smiled and headed for the swinging door that separated the kitchen from the dining room.

Her smile slipped a little as every eyebrow in the place rose in quiet speculation. Reaching for the coffee carafe, she filled the Anderson brothers' cups and moved on to the next table where Wes was in the process of taking a seat across from Boomer and DoraLee Brown.

"Mornin', Lou."

"Hi, Wes," she answered, her smile returning as he pulled another bouquet from behind his back. "You didn't have to bring me more flowers," she admonished, taking the pink carnations in her empty hand.

The dazed look Wes usually wore these days cleared. Eyeing her as if he was trying to figure something out, he said, "You alone in the kitchen?"

She glanced over her shoulder, catching DoraLee's eye on the way by. "Cletus is helping with the dishes. Why?"

"*Old* Cletus McCully?" Wes sputtered, his gaze homing in on her mouth.

"Is there a young Cletus McCully, sugar?" DoraLee asked.

As if deciding he must have imagined something, Wes said, "Aren't you gonna read the card?"

She placed the carafe on the table and opened the small card. "Roses are red. Daisies are sunny. You're much nicer than any rodeo bunny."

"That's sweet, Wes." She automatically placed her fingertips over her mouth, which in turn automatically reminded her of how her lips had tingled when Burke had kissed her. Suddenly flustered, she said something about putting the flowers in water and hurried into the kitchen. Thankful that Cletus was going about what he'd been doing, she took a moment to reorient herself. She was feeling much calmer by the time she took a pitcher off a shelf and filled it with water, adding the bouquet of flowers one stem at a time. "The coast's clear, Cletus. Gussie and Addie are gone."

"Hallelujah."

Eyeing all the clean dishes, she said, "No wonder they're both after you. Not only are you handsome and witty, but you do dishes, too."

Cletus McCully blanched. "If you're trying to rattle me, it's working."

"This must be the day for being rattled," she muttered under her breath. "Can I ask you something, Cletus?" she said, placing the pitcher filled with carnations on the counter.

He nodded his craggy head one time.

"Is my sweater on backward, or is my hair a mess, or have I grown a third eye or something?"

He looked her up and down as only a man could. "Your hair's a little windblown, and I ain't used to seeing it down around your shoulders, but everything seems to be in the right place. Why?"

"Well, everybody's looking at me as if—never mind."

Cletus slapped his towel on the counter. Making a *tsk, tsk, tsk* sound, he headed for the door. "You look fine. Pretty. Like a woman who's recently been thoroughly kissed."

The door swung closed behind him. This time it was Louetta who blanched.

She didn't move until the door had stopped swinging on its hinges. Merciful heavens. She *had* been thoroughly kissed. She'd had no idea it showed. No wonder everybody was looking at her strangely.

Louetta Graham simply didn't know how to handle this kind of attention, this kind of speculation. There was something to be said for being a wallflower, for blending in with the scenery. No, she told herself, putting the stacked dishes on the shelves where they belonged. Going unnoticed by people she'd known all her life had been a lonely way to exist. It had taken courage to make a stand three years ago. It had taken courage to dig her way out of her shell. She couldn't slide back in now, when she'd come so far.

The old Louetta would have taken the cowardly way out and stayed in the kitchen until everyone left. The new Louetta had no room in her life for craven tendencies and faintheartedness. Taking a deep breath, she pushed through the swinging door.

She let out a little yelp as a man swooped in front of her and pulled her to him the second she entered the room. "Wes," she exclaimed, watching in dismay as his face descended to hers.

His kiss had come out of the blue, which pretty much described the color of his eyes and the wink he gave her moments later. "There," he said, sauntering toward the door. "Might as well keep the gossips on their toes, don'tcha think? I'll see you tonight, Lou."

Louetta stared after him, one hand over her mouth, the

other over her heart. She knew her cheeks were flaming. And she knew everyone was looking at her. She couldn't bring herself to care.

Plain, shy Louetta Graham had gone thirty-three years without being kissed. Suddenly, at thirty-five, she'd been kissed by two of the most ruggedly attractive men in the entire state of South Dakota, and all in the span of fifteen minutes. Whatever was a woman to do?

"There I was," Wes Stryker said, blue eyes full of mischief as he regaled Louetta with another rodeo story, "balancin' on the top rung of the chute, all psyched to climb onto that bronco's back and stay there. Only, the horse had other ideas. And I knew, the second my butt hit the saddle, that I was in for quite a ride."

Louetta leaned forward in her chair, her stomach comfortably full, both hands curled around a cup of coffee, intrigued as much by the warmth and friendliness in Wes's expression as by the tale itself. "Did you last your eight seconds?" she asked, feeling her smile broaden at the look of self-confidence and humor on Wes's lean face.

"The longest eight and a half seconds of my life. Near as I can tell, ridin' a bucking bronco is a lot like steering a spaceship through reentry."

"How many times have you steered a spaceship through reentry?" Louetta asked around a grin.

Although she hadn't seen much of Wes since they'd graduated from high school, she realized he'd always been easy to be with. Maybe it was because he hadn't exactly fit in, either. He hadn't been unpopular, but he'd rarely participated in after-school activities.

Louetta couldn't remember much about Wes's mother, who'd died when he was a young boy, but it was common knowledge that Sam Stryker had had a drinking problem, just as it was common knowledge that the reason Wes had spent every free moment practicing his roping and riding skills was that he'd been planning his escape from Jasper Gulch. He'd left town the day after graduation. Although he'd come back a couple of times every year, nobody had really expected him to return for good. But then, Louetta thought to herself, nobody had ever expected her to be pursued by two men, either.

Holding his hand over his cup to let the passing waitress know he didn't want a refill, he wiggled his brows and said, "I've flown a biplane and driven a race car, but I can't say I've ever steered a spaceship into reentry. I *have* ridden plenty of broncos whose life ambition was to buck me off as fast and ungracefully as possible. You've gotta know where your center is when you're riding one of those creatures. And you've gotta know which way is up. Down is easy. And usually painful. You look real pretty tonight, Lou."

She toyed with the gold locket at her throat and tried to decide how to respond to the sudden change in topics. The man was full of surprises. The kiss he'd given her that morning in the diner had been a perfect example.

Wes appeared to enjoy the ensuing silence. Winking broadly, he said, "But then, you always were pretty."

Louetta's response to *that* was instinctive. She released a puff of air between pursed lips and rolled her eyes. "No wonder you're such a hit with rodeo fans. You can walk through knee-deep baloney without getting your boots dirty."

Several other patrons in the rustic steak house turned at the sound of Wes Stryker's laughter. "Hot dang, Louetta, you're better for what ails me than a hot compress and horse salve, and you're a whole lot easier on the nose and eyes."

Louetta lowered her lukewarm coffee to the table and rested her chin in her hand. Wes's words weren't romantic, but she didn't mind. It was easy to smile with him, and impossible to be offended by his simple praise.

"You probably say that to all the women you date."

The dazed expression crossing Wes's face reminded Louetta of a cloud passing over the face of the sun. For a moment his eyes had a burning, faraway look in them, causing her to wonder if there was more to his reason for coming back to Jasper Gulch than a sprained ankle and a few broken ribs. She wondered what he'd walked away from out on the rodeo circuit. Or who.

"Excuse me. Are you Louetta Graham?"

Louetta and Wes both glanced up at the waitress who had spoken. At Louetta's nod, the middle-aged woman handed her a small bouquet of flowers. "These just arrived for you."

Without conscious thought, Louetta brought the tiny bouquet to her nose. Inhaling the sweet scent of lilies of the valley, her eyes drifted closed and something went warm inside her.

"Who are they from?" Wes asked.

The tired-looking waitress shrugged. "Search me. I'm just the delivery person. Far as I know, there wasn't a card."

Louetta lowered the bouquet and met Wes's gaze across the table. There was only one person who would send her lilies.

"Dang," Wes said, a dawning look of understanding raising his eyebrows. "Score one point for the doctor." With an air of calm and self-confidence that had probably had a lot to do with how he'd won the trophies on the rodeo circuit, he added, "It looks like I'm gonna have to stay on my toes from now on."

Louetta lowered the flowers to the table. "Wes, I don't want things to get out of hand."

"Out of hand?" he declared, motioning for the check. "They're just gettin' interesting." Climbing stiffly to his feet, he grinned at her and dropped a few dollar bills on the table. "Don't worry. A little competition never hurt anybody. Least of all me."

"But, Wes, it isn't necessary..."

"If folks only did what was necessary, life would be no fun at all. Besides, you deserve the best. And you wanna have fun, don't you? Now, don't you worry about a thing. In fact, I want you to leave all the worrying to the good doctor and me."

Louetta refrained from telling Wes that *that* was going to be next to impossible. She felt a little sad, as if no one understood her. Not even Wes. Because if he had understood her, he would know that she wasn't doing this to have fun. And she certainly didn't want to be somebody's prize. She wanted to be loved, for who and what she was.

Pushing her chair out, she strode out of the steak house with Wes, the sweet scent of lilies of the valley wafting from the bouquet clutched tightly in her hand.

"Night, Lou."

"Good night." Louetta waved to Wes as he drove away. Still holding that bouquet of flowers in her hand, she turned toward her door, lost in thought.

Wes had been a perfect gentleman tonight. After walking her to her door, he'd tipped his hat back with one finger and kissed her good-night. He was tall and had a kind of ruggedness folks automatically associated with cowboys out here. He was really a very good kisser, even if his kiss hadn't curled her toes.

"Hello, Lily."

She glanced over her shoulder just in time to see a man dressed in black materialize out of the shadows. Her first instinct was to jump. Her second was much less easy to decipher. Her heart skipped a beat, her toes curling inside her brown shoes.

"Burke Kincaid, are you spying on me?"

His shoes crunched over loose gravel as he strode a few steps closer, the wind toying with his dark hair. "Just out for a late walk. Did you and Stryker have a good time?"

"Did Wes and I— Yes, yes, I suppose you could say we did. Wes is very easy to talk to." Although suddenly Louetta couldn't remember what they'd talked about.

Burke stopped less than two paces away. "I see you got my flowers."

She glanced at her hand, and then into Burke's face. "How did you know which steak house to send them to?"

"I sent a bouquet to every steak house in Pierre."

"You—" Glancing up at him, she told herself she wasn't reacting to the deep rumble in his voice, and she absolutely, positively forbade herself to give in to the hungry look deep in his hazel eyes.

"You didn't invite Stryker in. I'm assuming there's a good reason for that."

His voice brought back feelings that were as elusive as whispers in the wind. "People would talk," she said quietly.

"Did people talk about us two years ago?"

Louetta wished he hadn't reminded her of that other night, wished she could have forgotten how his leaving had hurt, how those first months without him had dragged into years. Mostly, she wished she could stop wishing. Telling herself to focus on his question, and not on the emotions his question evoked, she shook her head. "Other than Nick and Brittany Colter, who practically stumbled upon us as you were leaving the following morning, nobody knew.''

"Nobody?" Burke asked.

"I told one friend months later, and my mother before she died. But no, to this day, nobody else knows.''

Burke studied Lily's expression. Her eyes were open wide, the pupils so large in the semidarkness they appeared to be ringed by a narrow circle of gray. The light from the single bulb on a tall light pole barely reached this far. In the near darkness everything else took on shades of gray, as well—the shadow her eyelashes cast each time she blinked, her coat, the little hollow at the base of her neck, the flowers in her right hand.

"Stryker can give you all the carnations in the world," he said, shifting closer. "He can even give you roses, but lilies are the flowers that best suit you.''

He couldn't help noticing the way her throat convulsed on a swallow. Yet she didn't reply. She wasn't a woman for idle chatter. He'd learned that the first time he'd come here. When she *did* speak, it was of unpretentious things, important things. Most of the time, she listened. Consequently, a man had to pay close attention to her expressions, to the tilt of her head and the soft smiles that had a way of settling to her mouth.

His gaze strayed to her mouth. He remembered how her lips had felt, tasted, trembled beneath his. A need was growing inside him, making him increasingly aware that what he wanted to do right now didn't involve talking or listening. "Invite me inside," he whispered.

She took a backward step and slowly shook her head. "I don't think that would be a good idea.''

Burke didn't know why her statement bothered him. But it did. Lily wasn't like any other woman he'd ever known. The hold she had on him was strong, strong enough to last more than two years, quite possibly strong enough to last forever. Maybe that's what rankled—the fact that he didn't have as strong a hold on her. "Are you ashamed of what happened between us? Is that it?"

It required all the willpower Louetta possessed to keep her feet planted firmly where they were. "Ashamed?" she replied. "No, I'm not ashamed. It's just that it was so out of character for me I doubt anyone would have believed it."

In a jagged corner of her mind a voice whispered, *Of course they wouldn't have believed it.* Any proof she'd had was sadly gone.

He took a step closer, one hand reaching out to smooth a lock of hair away from her cheek. The shock of his touch kept her silent, but it seemed to have the opposite effect on Burke. "The men out here must be blind, but the wrong guy could take you for a rough ride."

Louetta studied his face unhurriedly. He had an angular jaw, masculine cheekbones and the eyes of a heartbreaker. She should know. She had the broken heart to prove it. Closing her eyes, she turned her head away from his touch. "Maybe the wrong guy already did."

Burke's hand dropped to his side through the still air. "I never meant to hurt you."

Gray eyes met hazel ones, two throats convulsing on things neither of them knew how to say. Burke was the first to find his voice. "Would you have dinner with me tomorrow night?"

She stared at him for a long time, her eyes dewy and deep. Finally she said, "I don't know. Seeing you again has complicated things, not to mention confused me."

Burke swore the beating rhythm of his heart changed tempo. Truth be told, he'd grown accustomed to complications years ago, and he wanted to confuse her, if it meant she would see him and give him a second chance.

"It's getting late," she said, breaking the silence.

Too late? he thought to himself. Unwilling to ask such a question too soon, he said, "I'll stop by the diner tomorrow morning. We can talk then."

She took a backward step. Before she could draw away completely, he kissed her. Not in the wild, frenzied way he'd kissed her before, but tenderly, sweetly, the way a woman like her deserved to be kissed. Raising his face from hers, he straightened the collar of her coat. "Good night, Lily. I'll see you tomorrow."

Louetta's mind reeled from that kiss. She might have been able to reply if he hadn't gone and done the last thing she expected. He smiled.

His smile dallied around the edges of her mind long after she'd climbed the stairs to her apartment and closed the door, long after she'd crossed her hands over her heart and slowly brought them to her face.

She started to pace. She started to sputter. Still, the memory of Burke's smile remained, bringing out every tender emotion she'd ever experienced, and a few brand-new ones.

This was a side of Burke she hadn't seen. The man was killing her with kindness, with gentleness and sweetness. She dropped onto her couch, only to spring to her feet almost instantly. She didn't have to act on these emotions. After all, she wasn't as naive as she'd once been. Whoever said "What doesn't kill us makes us stronger" knew what they were talking about.

Whether he had a gentle side or not, Burke had broken his promise to her when he'd failed to return when he said he would. In the process, he'd broken her heart. He hadn't written or called once in all this time, yet he seemed intent upon waltzing back into her life and picking up where they'd left off.

Touching her lower lip with the tip of one finger, she made a vow to herself. Before he kissed her again, she had to know why he hadn't come back two and a half years ago. And why he had now.

The bell jingled over the diner's door. "Goodness gracious, Louetta," Isabell declared, "it's Josie with another bouquet."

Louetta poked her head out the kitchen door, only to duck back inside for another vase. "Honestly," she said, bustling out into the nearly empty dining room again. "That's the fifth bouquet to arrive this morning. Wes has to stop spending all his..."

Her voice trailed away the instant she saw the yellow and orange daylilies in Josie Callahan's arms.

"Hurry, dear," Isabell insisted. "I can't wait to hear Wes's latest poem."

"Um, Isabell?" DoraLee Brown said in the ensuing silence. "I don't think these are from Wes."

"Whatever do you mean?"

Ignoring the question, DoraLee turned to Louetta. "They're from the new doctor, aren't they, sugar?"

Louetta pressed her cheek into the soft petals, nodding her head.

"How can you be so sure?" Isabell asked. "Why, Wes has been sending Louetta flowers all morning."

Flowers, Louetta thought to herself. Beautiful flowers in every color of the rainbow. But not lilies.

"I'm certain these are from Wesley, too. Just look at— Humph." Isabell's lips pursed the instant she read the card.

Louetta's glance at the masculine scrawl was automatic.

Sure enough, the card said nothing about roses being red or violets being blue. It was signed simply "Burke."

Placing the long-stemmed flowers in a vase she'd found on a high shelf, Louetta said, "Cletus thinks the diner's starting to look like a funeral parlor. I don't know how to make Burke and Wes stop."

"That's simple," DoraLee said. "Choose one."

"Not just any one," Isabell protested. "You need to choose our very own Wesley."

"It isn't that easy, is it, sugar?" DoraLee asked, looking at Louetta.

Isabell pounded a bony fist on the table in front of her. "That new doctor has terrible timing. Why, if he hadn't shown up when he did, Louetta here would be engaged to Wesley by now. Dr. Kincaid is trouble, with a capital *T*."

"Maybe," DoraLee said from the other side of the table, "but if I were younger, and not madly in love with Boomer, Dr. Kincaid would be exactly the kind of trouble I'd want to get into." The fifty-some-year-old bleached blonde winked at Louetta. "But then, there probably aren't too many gals who would complain if Wes put his cowboy boots under their beds, either."

"DoraLee, please," Isabell admonished. "Some of us don't appreciate such crudeness. Save the vulgarities for the patrons of your bar. Louetta and I are of gentler stock, aren't we, Louetta?"

Silence.

"Louetta?" Isabell asked.

Louetta paused, her nose in the bouquet of flowers that had just arrived. Meeting first Isabell's and then DoraLee's gaze, she placed the flowers on a nearby table. "I'm sorry. My mind must have wandered. What did you say?"

Before Isabell had a chance to repeat the question, DoraLee said, "Are you feeling all right, Louetta?"

"Yes, you haven't had another fainting spell, have you?" Isabell asked.

"I'm fine, really."

DoraLee eyed her shrewdly. "Wes moseyed into the bar a little after eleven, and Jake Monroe said that Forest Wilkie saw the new doctor talking to Ben Jacobs in front of the doctor's office right about the same time, so I know you weren't out late with either of them. You'd tell us if there was a third man in your life, wouldn't you?"

Isabell gasped, and Louetta exclaimed, "Two men are plenty, thank you."

DoraLee cast Louetta a meaningful look. "Eventually two men are going to be one man too many."

Isabell's pointy little chin bobbed in agreement. Fighting the urge to slide into a chair and rest her head on her arms, Louetta took up where she'd left off, cleaning the tables in her diner, thinking the three of them—the self-appointed leader of the Ladies Aid Society, the owner of the town's only bar and the shyest woman in the county—were an unlikely threesome. Although Isabell and DoraLee were on opposite sides of the fence on nearly every issue imaginable, they had one thing in common. They both held dear places in Louetta's heart.

For all her faults, Isabell had been like a second mother to Louetta all her life. The friendship Louetta shared with DoraLee had started a little over two years ago when DoraLee had overheard Louetta crying in the diner's kitchen late one night. Feeling sad and more alone than she'd ever felt in her life, Louetta had poured her heart out to the other woman.

The misery of that period in her life came back to haunt Louetta, squeezing like a fist around her heart just as the bell jingled over the door.

"Oh, no," Isabell declared.

"Oh, my," DoraLee said at the same time.

Louetta knew of only two things that could have such an opposite and instantaneous effect on the two other women. Either Josie was delivering another bouquet of lilies, or Burke Kincaid had just walked through the diner's front door.

Chapter Four

In the time it took Burke's eyes to adjust to the dim interior of the diner, Lily had turned to face him, and a woman with a long neck and pointy chin—he thought her name was Isabell—had risen to her feet, standing like a guard dog at her side.

"We stop serving breakfast at ten," the Olive Oyl look-alike said.

He shrugged out of his overcoat and took a moment to smile at the older woman. "I didn't come here for breakfast." Stealing a glance at Lily, he turned his smile up a notch. "Li—Louetta's expecting me."

"Louetta, is this true? Louetta?"

"Sugar?"

"Hmm?" Louetta came to her senses like a falling brick, with a thud a person could feel all the way to her toes. There was no use wondering what was happening to her concentration. Burke Kincaid could turn her inside out with just a look, but when he graced her with that smile, stark and white and full of shared promises and whispered secrets, her knees went weak and her resistance turned to mush. He wreaked havoc with her senses, no doubt about it.

That was it in a nutshell. She didn't understand him. But she understood what he did to her, how he made her feel. Glancing at the two women, who were watching Burke openly, Louetta said, "Isabell, I told Bonnie Trumble I'd try to stop in this morning to talk about a few of the songs we're going to have the children sing in the Christmas pageant later this month. I'm afraid I'm not going to be able to make it today. Would you mind poking your head inside the Clip & Curl and telling Bonnie for me?"

A pained expression crossed Isabell's narrow face, but she nodded and donned her drab coat. Once the bell had jingled, signaling her departure, Louetta turned to DoraLee. The bleached blonde held up one hand and slowly shook her head. "You don't have to invent an errand for me. I'm going, I'm going."

Moments later the bell jingled a second time. Suddenly Louetta and Burke were alone, and the diner was very quiet, and Louetta felt ill equipped to ask the questions she needed to ask.

Burke looked big and broad and dark. His eyes were steady, his gaze direct. She almost wished he would glance around, say something about the diner's decor, the faded awning out front and the checkered tablecloths that had seen better days. Then she could tell him that the ten tables and eight booths had been here since the diner opened more than fifty years ago. Maybe then the ice would be broken, and she would be able to broach the subject weighing so heavily on her mind.

Burke watched Lily's expression change with her changing thoughts. She was easy to read, and difficult to resist. Running a hand down the back of his neck, he finally broke the silence. "I happened to pass an old man sitting on the bench down on the corner. He said somebody named Josie's been delivering flowers here all morning. I recognize the lilies I just sent to you. Are the rest all from Stryker?"

She wet her lips and bravely met his gaze. "Does that bother you?"

Bother?

Burke took a deep breath. He'd passed bothered the second he'd seen Stryker go down on one knee and ask for Lily's hand two nights ago. "Why would it bother me? All's fair in love and war, right?"

Any other woman would have jumped at the opening he'd left her and asked which one of those things this was. Leave it to Lily to ignore the obvious and stride a few steps closer. "Burke, why did you come back to Jasper Gulch?"

He heard the soft rustle of her skirt, and imagined it swishing over silk and lace underneath. The thigh-high nylons she'd been wearing beneath her prim and proper dress two and a half years ago had been a pleasant surprise. The white shirt with its delicate pointed collar and the dark brown skirt that hugged her narrow hips this morning were more feminine than the clothes she'd been wearing on his first trip to Jasper Gulch. He couldn't help wondering if she still wore see-through bras and panties that fit in the palm of a man's hand. He was getting worked up just thinking about it. Heaven help him, he wanted to find out.

First, she deserved an honest answer to her question. Holding her gaze, he said, "I came to Jasper Gulch to practice medicine, to treat patients who were more than numbers on an insurance form. I came here because it felt right, and seemed like a good place to raise a family." A look of hurt he didn't understand crossed her face, and caused him to add, "And because no matter how hard I tried, I've never been able to forget."

"Then you wanted to forget?"

Burke crossed his arms, only to uncross them and place his hands on his hips. Hell, if he could have forgotten, life would have been a lot easier. He strode to the counter, where a basket of apples sat next to an old-fashioned cash register. Eyes narrowed, he turned and faced Lily once again. "I don't normally take my love on the run. Believe it or not, the night I stayed here with you was a once-in-a-lifetime experience. Just thinking about it heats up certain regions on my body."

"Regions?"

God, he loved it when her voice went all soft and shivery. It lowered his own voice, and drew him closer. "Nether regions. Traitorous nether regions that are catching fire as I speak."

Louetta absolutely positively forbade her gaze to browse any lower then Burke's shoulders. She couldn't do anything about the blush heating her cheeks, or the image forming in her mind, but she could do something about what was going to happen if she didn't put a stop to his forward motion.

Raising her hand, she said, "Hold it right there."

"That's what I was hoping you'd say."

The huskiness in Burke's voice faded to a hushed stillness, filtering past the flimsy barricade she'd placed around her heart. She spun around, zigzagging around tables that would soon be filled with the usual lunch crowd.

"When you didn't return," she said, talking as she went, "I swore I'd never let you hurt me again, never let you close, never *want* to let you close. I mean, I still had my pride, right? I have my diner, and lately I've had the attention of a really nice guy who wouldn't be a bad catch for a girl like me."

Burke lessened the distance between them with long,

purposeful strides. As if something about her statement didn't add up, he said, "What do you mean, for a girl like you? You deserve more than a little pride and a nice guy you don't love."

Louetta stopped in her tracks and released a long breath of air. Burke was standing in *her* diner, looking for all the world as if he belonged there, and all she could think about was being crushed in his arms. Obviously, her heart didn't know the meaning of the word *pride*. "You play dirty, doctor."

"Louetta?" he said, letting the name roll off the tip of his tongue. "This isn't a game to me. It never was."

She closed her eyes, wanting to believe him. When she opened them again, he was staring at her mouth, his face steadily descending to hers, his lips parting slightly on a ragged breath.

"Doctor!"

The door burst open. And Louetta and Burke jerked apart.

"Jason!" Louetta called. "What is it?"

"It's Boomer," shouted Jason Tucker, one of the area ranch hands. "He's hurt real bad."

Burke was already racing toward the door. "My bag's in my car. I'm parked out front. Let's go."

Louetta grabbed Burke's overcoat as she followed him and Jason out the door. A few of the old-timers who'd noticed the commotion from Ed's Barbershop came a-running. "What happened?" somebody called.

"It's Boomer," Jason answered. "He needs a doctor right away."

"Did he get gored by that new bull?"

"Dragged by his horse?"

"Tangled up in barbed wire?"

Jason shook his head. "He fell off the roof he was mending. Jed Harley saw him laying in a heap on the ground and called Doc Masey's office, but there was nobody there.''

"Doc's checking on Karl Hanson," Burke said, reaching into the back seat for his bag.

"I know," Jason answered. "Crystal told me. She said you were in the diner."

Louetta was holding the door for Burke when he straightened. "How far away is Boomer's ranch?" he asked.

"Only eight miles," Louetta answered. "But it's all back roads and hidden turns. It's not easy to find."

"Then you drive."

"You wanna get there in one piece?" somebody called.

"Then you'd better find somebody else to drive," someone else added.

"Shoot, Doc Kincaid," Jason Tucker cut in sheepishly. "Everybody knows Louetta makes a great peach pie, and her chili's every bit as good as Melody's was. But she's never been behind the wheel of an automobile in her life. Ain't that right, Louetta?"

Louetta met Burke's gaze. She knew her cheeks were flaming, and she almost gave in to the impulse to hang her head. Catching herself in the nick of time, she kept her chin level and her gaze direct. "That's right, Jason," she said in a voice so quiet she was amazed he heard, "you take Burke to Boomer's place. I'll tell DoraLee."

"Call for an ambulance," Burke said, climbing into Jason Tucker's muddy truck.

Louetta nodded again. With her heart in her throat, she handed Burke his overcoat and watched him and Jason spin away toward Boomer's ranch. While Cletus ran inside the diner to call an ambulance, Louetta ran across the street to tell DoraLee that the husband she adored had been hurt.

* * *

"He fell off the roof, you say?"

"What was he doing mending the roof when nobody else was around?"

"You know Boomer. Even before he convinced DoraLee to marry him, he thought he could do anything."

"Yeah? Well, I guess he learned the hard way that he can't fly."

"You know what they say. The bigger they are, the harder they fall."

Louetta turned a deaf ear to the gossip swirling around her. Carafe in hand, she walked around the diner refilling coffee cups and serving dessert.

"I heard DoraLee threatened to kill him if he so much as thought about dying on her."

"I heard that Doc Kincaid was amazing."

Louetta tensed, her breath solidifying in her throat at the mention of Burke's name. Cletus McCully winked at her and, bless his heart, didn't bat an eye when the slice of pie she was serving landed upside down on his plate. When she moved to take it away, he covered her hand with his gnarled fingers and said, "Don't you fret, girl. Your piecrusts are so good it don't matter if the pie is upside down or right side up."

Trying valiantly to smile, she strode to the counter where the old Everts brothers were waiting to pay for their meals. "Boomer got lucky this time. Sounds like he has a slight concussion and a broken leg. Both will heal. But a scare like this makes a person stop and think," seventy-two-year-old Hal said.

"Ain't that the truth," Roy declared. "If a strong, barrel-chested young fella like Boomer can come this close to meetin' his Maker, just think how close we're gettin'."

Louetta punched the Sale button on the cash register.

Rather than mentioning that the *strong young fella* they were talking about was thirty-nine, she handed Hal his change and said, "You two are going to live another twenty or thirty years at least."

"Maybe. Maybe not," Hal insisted. "But I know one thing. Doc Masey knew what he was doin' when he brought the new doctor into his practice. I hear tell Doc Kincaid peeked in Boomer's eyes, took his vitals and had him stabilized in almost no time at all. It seems the man's a genius with his hands."

Louetta glanced around, amazed and slightly shaken that nobody else had picked up on the double entendre in Hal's simple statement. If she'd been anybody else, the local cowboys and ranchers would have nudged one another, commenting that she probably already knew just how good Burke was with his hands.

She knew she had no right to be disappointed. For heaven's sake, women shouted sexual harassment for lesser things. She didn't want to be harassed. She didn't really want to be the butt of jokes, either. She just wanted to be accepted for who and what she was. It seemed that despite all the strides she'd made these past three years, the folks of Jasper Gulch still saw her as the prim and proper daughter of the former church organist, the girl voted most likely not to, by her fellow classmates.

By the time the last few stragglers had finished their lunches and had moseyed out the door, Louetta's dander was up. *Sure. Louetta Graham could make a mean batch of chili and a tasty pie, but don't expect her to know how to drive a car, and, whatever you do, don't think of her as a normal woman with a normal woman's needs and desires.*

It wasn't that she wanted a bad reputation. She just couldn't understand why cowboys and ranchers she'd known all her life couldn't see beneath her shyness, where there lurked the heart of a passionate woman who had hidden thoughts and dreams and fantasies.

She was draining the dishwater the first time she heard a horn honk outside. When the sound came again and again and again, she went to the front window and peered out.

"What the—" She dried her hands on her apron and was out the door before the horn sounded again.

"Burke Kincaid, what are you doing?"

Burke was parked in front of the diner, his window down, the heat in his eyes at odds with the cold wind blowing through Louetta's thin shirt and skirt. Taking his hand from the horn, he finally said, "Get in."

"What?"

He started to slide over, and she had to lean closer to see and hear him. "Get in."

Eyeing the steering wheel and the driver's seat he was vacating, she said, "What are you doing, Burke?"

"It's high time you learned to drive. Consider this your first lesson."

There was an invitation in the depths of his hazel eyes, and a smoldering awareness in the gaze trained on hers. She glanced over the roof of his expensive black car. Just as she'd suspected, Burke's horn-honking had stirred up a lot of interest up and down Main Street. Cletus McCully was standing in front of the barbershop with a group of old-timers. Edith Ferguson and Bonnie Trumble were gawking from the doorway of Bonnie's Clip & Curl, and Luke Carson and Wyatt McCully had stridden to the curb in front of the Jasper Gulch Animal Clinic to see what the commotion was about.

"What's the matter?" Burke asked, drawing her attention. "Hasn't anyone ever offered to teach you how to drive?"

"No," she said, shivering. "Nobody ever has."

"Well?" That one little word was chock-full of challenge.

She wavered in indecision.

"Are you going to stand there in the cold all day? Or do you want to learn to drive?"

She cast a quick glance at her diner. The lights were on inside, but nobody would mosey in for another two hours, at least. That meant she had time for a daring adventure. The question was, did she have the nerve?

Yes. Yes, indeed, she had the nerve. If she hurried, that is, and didn't give in to the doubts and fears that had hindered her for as long as she could remember.

She removed her apron, opened the door and slid inside before she could change her mind. This is it, she thought, a wild and crazy sense of giddiness chasing the goose bumps up and down her spine. Another step out of her shell.

Burke leaned over her, pushing a button that sent her window gliding closed. He removed his finger from the control, but he didn't straighten or pull away. His face was inches from hers, his shoulder touching her arm, his right hand on the seat near her thigh. For a moment everything else disappeared—all her shyness, all the people watching, all her misgivings. For a moment there was only the two of them, alone in a luxurious car. For a moment she was Lily again, sure of herself, of her sensuality, and of the man before her.

The moment passed, and the real Louetta Graham resurfaced, along with all her misgivings. "Your reputation is already ten feet tall," she said quietly. "Talk is all over town about the way you diagnosed Boomer's injuries and had him bustled off in an ambulance in almost no time at all. Are you sure you want to take a chance on teaching me to drive on such a red-letter day?''

Burke studied Lily's face unhurriedly, feature by feature. The wind had put color on her cheeks, but it was an inner turmoil that darkened her gray eyes to the color of smoke. She was hauntingly beautiful. He'd seen it the first time they'd met, and remembered wondering how the men out here had failed to notice all these years. Today's emergency had brought out his lightning-quick reflexes. In the aftermath of that adrenaline rush, a few things about Lily had become clear. These men had grown up with her. They took her for granted, just as they took her beauty and inner warmth for granted. Burke could live with that. What he couldn't live with was the way she saw herself.

How many times had he heard her say, ''He's a good catch for a girl like me''? He'd picked up bits and pieces of conversations about her childhood, about the father who had adored her but who'd died when she was small, and the overprotective mother who had raised her. ''Shy, plain Louetta.'' That was how more than one of the Jasper Gents had referred to her.

There had been nothing shy about her the first time they'd met. One look into those deep gray eyes, and he'd been lost. One touch of her hand, one whisper-soft brush of her lips on his, and he'd had to have her. Need burrowed deep inside him at the memory alone. Wind howled outside his car. But here, inside, he and Lily were warm. And all alone.

''Tell me what to do.''

For the span of one heartbeat, Burke thought his fantasies were coming true. He imagined coaxing her to shift ever closer, to place her hand just so, and her lips on his.

''You're not moving. Does that mean you aren't sure you want to do this?'' she whispered.

The question sent cymbals crashing inside his head, and desire pooling low in his body.

"I mean," she said, wetting her lips, "are you insured for this?"

Insured?

Realization dawned. Driving. She was talking about driving, not kissing him senseless, and unbuttoning his shirt, and unfastening his pants, and—

His vision cleared just as a second set of cymbals crashed inside his skull. "Never ask a doctor about insurance," he said, his voice sounding husky in his own ears. "And Louetta? I'm thrilled at the thought of being your first. Again."

She swallowed nervously. It was all he could do to keep from pressing his lips to the smooth column of her throat and coaxing the nerves right out of her. Forcing himself back to reality, he returned to his own bucket seat and said, "Turn the key in the ignition."

Her fingers shook slightly, but the expensive engine turned over like a cat purring in a patch of sunshine.

"That's it. Now put your foot on the brake, and ever so gently pull the lever into Reverse."

The transmission shifted into Reverse, causing Lily to jump.

"Now take your foot off the brake and press the gas pedal lightly."

He almost smiled at the way she slammed her foot back on the brake the instant she felt the car begin to move.

"Try it again," he said. "Nobody's coming. See? There aren't many obstacles between here and the village limits. Once we're out in the country, all you'll have to do is keep it between the ditches."

She clutched the steering wheel so tightly her knuckles turned white. "Atta girl," he said as they slowly headed down Main Street. "Now see if you can get her to go faster than five miles per hour."

"Oh-my-gosh! Oh-my-gosh! Oh-my-gosh! I'm driving. Burke, I'm really driving."

Burke settled himself more comfortably in his seat and glanced at Lily's profile. Wavy tendrils of hair had escaped a wide barrette at her nape. Although her jaw was set nervously, her lips were wide and full, and a smile was trying to poke out of its hiding place.

"I'm doing it!"

He nodded.

And she glanced at him. "I'm really and truly doing it."

He nodded a second time, his smile slipping a notch when they came dangerously close to a mailbox on his side.

"Oops," she said, righting the car and keeping her eyes trained on the road.

"It's all right. You're doing great."

"I am, aren't I?" And then, with more wonder, "I really and truly am. Look at me. Plain, shy Louetta Graham can do anything. I can drive a car, run a restaurant. I can even keep my vow to refrain from kissing you. Yahoo! I can do anything I put my mind to."

The cymbals in Burke's head crashed a third time.

They drove on in silence, an old country-western tune playing on the radio. His heart beat a heavy rhythm in perfect time to the music, but his mind hadn't fully recovered from her mention of a vow to refrain from kissing him.

He was aware of Lily's every movement, and he knew the exact moment she forced herself to take a deep breath and loosen her grip on the steering wheel. She conquered turning after one bout of oversteering. It seemed she was an avid listener and a very fast learner. Of course, he'd discovered that the first night he'd spent in Jasper Gulch.

"There's the bridge over Sugar Creek," she said, pulling the car to a stop so fast they both jerked forward in their seats.

"Why did you stop?" he asked, his voice a low rumble in the quiet car. *And what the hell did you mean, you aren't going to kiss me again?*

She glanced at him, and then at the bridge that was covered with a layer of fluffy white snow. "Nobody's coming," he said. "Come on, Lily. You can do it. Just aim for the middle."

Her knuckles were white again on the steering wheel, and Burke was pretty sure he could have walked across the bridge faster than Louetta drove, but there was no disguising her sigh of relief and wonder when she reached the other side. She pulled to a stop, put the shifting lever in Park and turned around to look at the progress she'd made, the distance she'd come.

"Driving isn't as hard as it looks. Maybe the next time there's an emergency, I'll be able to help."

"You did help," he said, his face close to hers. "You made sure an ambulance was called, and you told DoraLee. Both of those things had to be done."

Louetta's heart was beating hard, as if she'd just run a marathon. Staring behind her at the tracks the tires had left in the snow, she took a deep breath. Feeling slightly wobbly, but on safer ground, she said, "Yes, but you have no idea how it feels to be scared of everything, to have to force yourself to take even the tiniest baby step. I'm hardly what you'd call a dreamer, but it hurts to be overlooked and taken for granted."

"I don't take you for granted, Lily."

Her eyes met his. Suddenly she thought it was highly possible that learning to drive on roads covered with a layer of new snow hadn't required as much strength as resisting the urge to bring her hand to his lean cheek. Her gaze got caught on his long-lashed hazel eyes, on the high cheek-bones that made him look aristocratic, on the mouth that made him look the tiniest bit devilish and daring.

She couldn't help herself. She touched the corner of his lips with the tip of one finger. "You have a poet's mouth."

"And you said you're not a dreamer."

It was just like him to say the one thing in all the world that melted her insides, that sent her emotions into a wild swirl and made her almost forget her newest resolve. She glanced behind her, and then in front of her, before asking, "How far do you want to go?"

"I beg your pardon?"

Louetta felt a strange compulsion to grin. *Burke* had heard the double entendre. It was there in the huskiness in his voice. He was different than the men out here. It wasn't just the way he dressed, or the way he walked. She'd been surrounded by rugged cowboys and ranchers all her life, and yet not one of them stirred her senses and interpreted her words in a sexual, sensual way. Only Burke did that.

"How far do you want to go in the car?" She wet her lips and tried again. "Er, I mean, with the driving lesson. How far do you want me to drive your car?"

Burke stayed where he was, trying to gain control of his breathing, not to mention his rampaging hormones. He supposed Lily's reaction had been automatic. The nervous flick of her tongue over her dry lips and the flutter of her hands that she'd grasped tightly together in her lap had probably been instinctive, just as *his* reaction to the heat in her eyes had an automatic and profound effect on his body. Clearing his throat, he said, "I guess we can go as far as you want to go."

Her gaze flew to his. Suddenly she smiled. "That just

goes to show you a person should be careful what she wishes for.''

''What are you wishing for?'' he asked.

She stared over his shoulder, out the window on his side, into the distance where Sugar Creek made a sharp curve toward the west. ''There are so many things I want to try. Do you realize I've never been naughty in my life? Well, other than that night you ran out of gas, and one other time when I borrowed some pretty underclothes that were hanging on Lisa and Jillian's clothesline. It was awful. Lisa thought someone had stolen them, and I was so embarrassed I tried to put them back without anyone knowing it. Lisa and Wyatt McCully caught me red-handed. Even though Lisa gave me the articles of clothing as a gift, I'd never been more mortified in my life. You see, I've never had my mouth washed out with soap. I've never even been grounded. Why, the eleven-year-old girl who comes into the diner to wash dishes after school has been naughtier than me. Haley Carson's tamed down a lot since her father married Melody McCully, but the girl is still a hundred times more daring than I am. She went skinny-dipping when she was nine years old. What I wouldn't give for a little bit of that kind of nerve.''

Burke's mind was still reeling from her earlier declaration about kissing him. Or more specifically about *not* kissing him. Her mention of pretty underclothes nearly did him in. Holding Lily's gaze, he said, ''I'd say it's a little cold for skinny-dipping. But if you're game, let's go.''

Her head jerked around, her gaze meeting his, only to dart away again. She glanced at the creek bank, at the snow and then at the skirt she was wearing. Good Lord, Burke thought. She was thinking about it.

''I have to warn you, Lily,'' he said huskily. ''If we go skinny-dipping, I *will* be kissing you.''

He heard her breath catch in her throat, saw her waver in indecision before raising her chin proudly. "I think I'd better start with something a little less naughty. And Burke? I intend to keep my vow not to kiss you. At least until after you've told me the truth about why you didn't come back until now."

She held his gaze bravely, but Burke wasn't fooled. Her fingers quivered, her entire body vibrating like a small animal trapped by a hunter. No, he thought to himself. Not like a trapped animal. More like a sparrow perched on the edge of its nest, ready to fly, but terrified of taking that first leap into thin air.

He'd gotten to know *Lily* intimately well. But he was only just beginning to know the side of her everyone else called Louetta. She was beautiful, and endearingly shy. He loved that side of her, but she didn't. She wanted more. She was on the verge of reaching out, of conquering, of taking her first solo flight. Would she still do it if he told her the truth?

The truth was stark. Painful.

He'd wanted to return. God, how he'd wanted to. He'd never faced such a difficult decision in his life. He'd made his choice. And he'd tried not to look back. Because he'd known, even then, that he couldn't have lived with himself if he'd chosen any other way.

He stared at Lily, into eyes that could jump-start his heart and send need crashing through him. He tried to put his thoughts in order, tried to form an answer, tried to find a way to tell her...

But he couldn't tell her. Could he?

How did a man tell a woman as beautiful and sensitive as Louetta that the reason he hadn't returned two and a half years ago was that he'd married someone else?

Chapter Five

Burke looked out the window on Lily's side of the car, at the landscape that stretched as far as the eye could see. It was only the middle of the afternoon, but it seemed later. It probably had something to do with the fact that there were only a few weeks left before the shortest day of the year. The sky was gray, the sun was going, and so was the day. It reminded Burke of the winter he'd turned twenty and had driven across country in search of something fleeting, something that had been missing from his life. He'd been on his way home, dejected because he hadn't found what he'd been looking for, and had gotten as far as Arizona when he'd decided to follow the setting sun. He'd ended up along the coast of California just as the sun was dropping into the Pacific Ocean. Watching as darkness claimed the sky, he'd witnessed the end of the day, and heard it, and felt it.

With his feet in the cool sand, ocean water soaking his pant legs, he'd discovered that a person couldn't find what was missing from his life by searching the outside. It had to come from within. He'd started medical school as soon as he'd returned to Washington, but he'd never felt the end of a day quite the way he'd felt that one. Until now. And he'd certainly never longed for darkness to fall the way he did now. More than anything else, he'd never longed to hold a woman in that darkness the way he longed to hold Lily today.

Could he tell her he loved her in one breath, and in the next make her understand what it had cost him to marry a woman he'd cared about but hadn't loved, a woman who'd tricked him? Denise might not have been a saint, but she'd loved him. How many people in love did the wrong thing for the right reasons? She'd lived with her guilt for two years, and hadn't deserved to die of an aneurism soon after her thirty-second birthday. But then, when did death ever have anything to do with just deserts?

And what would the knowledge do to Lily's fledgling determination and yearning to soar?

She was huddled next to the door, holding perfectly still, waiting. If he told her, would she still take to the air? Or would his declaration slice her heart wide open and send her back into the relative safety of her small apartment and the life she'd always lived?

Burke squeezed his fingers into fists at his sides. He didn't know what to do. Was he being selfish? Or was his wish for Lily, or Louetta, honorable? Maybe he should just blurt out the truth and see what happened.

Would she run straight into Stryker's arms?

She didn't love Stryker. Burke knew it as surely as he knew his own name. That didn't mean she wouldn't marry the ex-rodeo champion. She would try to tell herself it wouldn't be so bad. But Burke knew firsthand how empty such an existence could be.

He made his decision. He would tell her. Just as soon as he was sure she wouldn't backpedal into her shell.

Shifting toward her, he smoothed a wavy lock of hair away from her cheek. "I had a very good reason, and some day I'll explain. I promise. In the meantime, I'd be happy to help you be naughty. But I have to tell you, *not* kissing you is going to be one hell of a challenge."

Louetta stared into Burke's eyes. He wasn't going to tell her what had happened to change his mind and his plans two and a half years ago. Darn him for sitting there and smugly offering to help her be naughty. Darn him for causing her traitorous mind and heart to contemplate the possibilities despite that fact.

Darn him, darn him, darn him.

"We should probably be getting back." His voice sounded deep, sensuous, *trustworthy*.

Darn him for that, too.

She'd felt as if she was walking on eggshells for days. And she'd had enough. Enough.

"Are you ready?" he asked.

She faced straight ahead. "To drive back to Jasper Gulch?"

"To accept the challenge."

"What challenge?" she asked, her gaze swinging to his despite her resolve to give him a cold shoulder and the silent treatment.

"You're the one who vowed *not* to kiss me. You've got a supper crowd to feed. Why don't you come to my place after you've closed up so you can practice *not* kissing me. I'll cook."

"You can cook?" She almost crossed her eyes and stuck her tongue out at herself. Did she have no pride?

"I can cook well enough to keep from starving. What

do you say? Opportunity's knocking. Are you ready to answer?''

She stared at him, speechless.

"What's the matter? Are you chicken?"

Bawk, buck, buck, buck. Bawk, buck, buck, buck.

Her shoulders went back and her chin came up. "Who, me?''

Without another word she put the car in gear and slowly drove toward town.

"Come on in!" Burke's deep voice sounded muffled, as if it was coming from another room.

Okay, Louetta admitted, opening his front door a crack, she *was* afraid. Terrified was more like it. She was also angry at herself for her cowardly ways. Bristling, she gave the door a shove. "Burke?"

"I'll be right there," he called. "Just as soon as I stir this sauce.''

She stomped the slush from her boots on the mat, closed the door behind her and peered around. She'd been in this very room only yesterday, when she'd cleared her conscience and told Burke that her nickname really used to be Lily. That had been in broad daylight. It was almost eight o'clock right now, and already pitch-dark outside. Normally, the ground was covered with a layer of snow by early December, which would have helped illuminate the way. But the weather was having a hard time making up its mind this year. As a result of the higher than normal temperatures, the snow that had fallen yesterday had melted and the wind felt more like springtime, which made it difficult to get into the holiday festivities and admire lighted Christmas trees and reindeers' red noses.

She was in the process of unbuttoning her coat when

Burke's voice called again. "Make yourself at home. I'll be right with you."

She hung her coat on a coat tree in the corner, then meandered from one corner of the living room to the other. Burke had been unpacking a box when she'd been here yesterday. Today the box was gone and the shelves were full of thick volumes of medical books.

Surely people didn't actually *read* such monstrosities, did they? she thought, leafing through one particularly thick volume. Placing the book back on the shelf, she peered into the next room, where a table was set with red place mats and white dishes. Good Lord. She couldn't believe she'd actually agreed to have dinner with Burke.

What had she been thinking?

Maybe if she'd had more experience with men, she would know how to stand up for herself and insist that he tell her the truth. Maybe if she'd had more experience, she would know how to while away the time waiting in the living room. Too bad she could fit all her experience with men into one weekend.

Don't think about that weekend.

The smell of wood smoke was in the air, along with the tangy scent of spaghetti sauce. Her stomach rumbled with hunger, the crackle of a fire drawing her into the dining room. The fire was hypnotic, and just a lick of flames at first. It crackled and snapped as it climbed over kindling. With a whoosh that sent her reeling backward, the first pine log caught fire.

"I hope you like spaghetti."

She glanced over her shoulder. Burke was leaning in the doorway, a checkered towel thrown over one shoulder, a pair of dark dress slacks slung low on his hips, a white turtleneck sweater hugging his upper torso like a second skin. He was in his stocking feet. And Louetta was glad she'd left her boots on. The two-inch heels put her on more equal ground with Burke's gaze. If the nerves fluttering in the pit of her stomach were an accurate indication, she needed all the help she could get.

"Who doesn't like spaghetti?" she asked.

"That's what I was hoping you'd say." He turned on his heel and headed back the way he'd come. Louetta didn't know what to do except follow. She stopped in the kitchen doorway, leaning in the exact place he'd been moments ago.

Music wafted from a portable CD player on top of an old refrigerator, a mellow folk song covering the quiet. She glanced at the speakers, and then at Burke's back, wondering if his choice in music was a coincidence. Or had he remembered that this mellow song about the Smoky Mountains was her favorite song?

"Something smells good," she said, for lack of anything better to say.

She'd known hours ago what Burke was fixing. His trip to the JP Grocery had been all over town minutes after he'd left with his spaghetti sauce, frozen strawberries and store-bought shortcakes.

He tossed the towel to the counter and stirred a pot of bubbling liquid on the stove, the jar it had come in sitting on the counter nearby. "I can microwave anything. And as long as I cook simple things I can usually keep the smoke alarm from going off."

Steam rose from a pot on the stove. Removing the lid, he dropped in a handful of uncooked spaghetti. He peered into the box, and then into the pot. "I never know how much of this to make."

She nodded, and felt herself beginning to smile. "Pasta can really get away from you."

He turned, easing into a smile of his own. Louetta felt

her throat constrict. Just being in the same room with him sent anticipation and a heady sense of urgency racing through her. It was easy to get lost in the way he looked at her. Too easy.

"Is there anything I can do to help?" she asked, miffed at herself for sounding so breathless.

He was shaking a can of whipped topping when he answered. "Actually," he said, tipping the can upside down and pushing the nozzle, "I think I have everything under control."

Artificial whipped cream spurted out of the can, spraying the counter, Burke's sweater and the back of his hand. Louetta hurried toward him, grabbing the towel he'd flung on the counter on her way by. His hand hovered close to his mouth, as if he was going to lick the topping off. Their eyes met, and ever so slowly he lowered his hand, offering the sweet cream to her.

Neither of them moved. In the space so near him, Louetta couldn't think of a single thing to do or say. Burke seemed to have no such problem. His breath came in deep drafts, his eyes holding her spellbound, his voice a husky whisper as he murmured, "It's all yours, Louetta. You said you wanted to be naughty."

Louetta tried to square her shoulders against his allure. It worked, for about two seconds. Then that devil-may-care grin of his got hold of her sensibilities, and suddenly she wanted to throw caution to the wind, to have a little fun and be a little daring. She reached for his hand and slowly brought it to her lips.

Burke felt the first tentative touch of Lily's fingertips, the shy flick of her tongue. The air whooshed out of him when she opened her mouth over the back of his hand and slowly closed her lips over the whipped topping.

Her eyelashes fluttered, then rose, her gray eyes bravely

meeting his. The look in her eyes nearly buckled his knees; the blood pounding through his head sounded like a freight train.

He felt her draw away from him, and had to stop himself from grasping her shoulders and hauling her into his arms. With a lift of one eyebrow, he brought a finger to his cheek where a dollop of cream had landed. She shook her head and deftly handed him the kitchen towel.

"Spoilsport," he said, swiping the towel across his face.

She smiled. And Burke sucked in a ragged breath. There was something different about her, something that hadn't been present two years ago. It wasn't her smile. She slanted that at nearly everyone she knew. It wasn't the light brown color of her hair. It wasn't even the mascara on her eyelashes or the gloss on her lips. It was something else. Something beyond the ordinary, and far deeper than a slight dusting of powder or the scent of her shampoo.

What was it? The tilt of her head? The paleness of her cheeks? That was it—what was different about her. She wasn't blushing.

"I can't believe I did that," she said, coyly meeting his gaze.

Burke hadn't been certain she would do it, either. When it came to Lily, he wasn't certain of anything. But how could he *not* believe she'd kissed the sweet cream off the back of his hand when he had living proof in the exact place her lips had nuzzled, tickled, tasted? It required every ounce of restraint he possessed to keep his hormones in check.

As if she was oblivious to the turn his thoughts had taken, she said, "I never realized appalling behavior could be so much fun."

They shared a long, meaningful look. In that instant Burke knew the discomfort was worth it. This was his first glimpse of the young girl who was still inside her. It made him want to see more.

"Would you tell me something?" he asked.

At her nod, he said, "You mentioned something today during your driving lesson, and, well, it made me curious."

"What did I say?"

"You said you've never been naughty in your life, except the weekend you spent with me, and the time you borrowed lacy underclothes from a friend's clothesline. For the record, I don't consider what we did naughty. It was incredible and complicated and beautiful, not to mention sensual as hell. Like you..."

Louetta held perfectly still. She couldn't help it. There was a current in his voice, like a taut rope being played by one finger, strumming it into a low, mellow hum. It reminded her of how he'd sounded his first night here, when he'd discovered her passion, and the thigh-high nylons she'd been wearing underneath her plain dress. In some far corner of her mind she heard the quick ding of a timer. She couldn't bring herself to pay it any mind, not with the way the blood was draining out of her face, and the way heat was gathering around her heart, slowly radiating all the way down to the tips of her toes.

"Do you still like folk music?" he asked.

Through the roaring din in Louetta's ears, she tried to make sense of the question. She'd been sure he was going to ask her something far more personal than that. Perhaps something pertaining to the way they'd fallen into bed that long-ago night, or if she still had a passion for skimpy panties and lacy bras.

"You want to know if I still like folk music? That's what you wanted to ask?"

His gaze homed in on her cheeks. "What did you think I was going to ask?"

She bit her lip, stammered for a few seconds and finally blurted, "I thought you were going to ask me if I still wear black satin and see-through lace."

He took a step toward her, pinning her in place with his gaze, a hand resting on the counter on either side of her. "Do you?"

She'd promised herself she wouldn't fall prey to his wiles until he leveled with her. Even while she'd been telling herself to withstand his charms, she'd been imagining his expression should he ever see what was underneath her simple blue dress. She wasn't imagining the wild swirl in the pit of her stomach right now, or the heat emanating from Burke's hazel eyes.

"Well?" he asked.

She might have nodded, or she might have simply hummed an answer. She would never know which, but she doubted she would ever forget the open look of longing on Burke's face. No matter what her resolve had been, this man made her feel things no other man had ever made her feel. He brought out emotions and responses and yearnings no other man had ever brought out in her. And he remembered that she loved folk music.

He lowered his head a few inches, drawing down as she was being drawn up, up, until there were mere centimeters separating their lips, mere centimeters separating their bodies. She knew there was something she was supposed to recall, something she'd promised herself she wouldn't do. Funny, she couldn't seem to concentrate, couldn't seem to draw more than a shallow breath as she waited for Burke's lips to touch hers.

A horrendous beep split the air.

Louetta jerked back, heart in her throat.

Smoke billowed around the oven door, straight into the smoke alarm's sensors. She vaguely remembered that a timer had gone off a few minutes ago. While Burke swiped the towel off the counter, opened the oven and grabbed a pan of charred dinner rolls, she rushed to open a window. With a flick of her wrist she turned on the overhead fan.

Just like that, the beeping stopped, and Burke and Louetta stood shoulder to shoulder, staring at the charred remains of what was supposed to be part of their dinner.

"I thought you said your cooking didn't make the smoke alarm go off."

She felt his shrug against her arm. "I said my cooking doesn't *usually* make the smoke alarm sound."

His words drew her gaze, the subtle look of amusement in his eyes making her smile. "You really can't cook."

He shook his head, and she started to laugh. And so did he. Before long they were holding on to each other, stomachs heaving, chests aching from the laughter bubbling there. Louetta realized that no other man had ever made her laugh like this, either.

It seemed like a long time before their laughter finally trailed away. When it did, she found herself pressed to Burke's chest, his arms around her back, her face nestled in the crook of his neck. He smelled good. A little like whipped cream, a little like burned bread, a lot like man.

She lifted her head and found him watching her. Neither of them moved for a long time. And then he said, "Consider yourself *almost* kissed."

Her eyelids fell, her breath sticking in her throat. Since she couldn't very well stand in Burke's kitchen indefinitely without moving or making a sound, she walked to the stove and began to stir the spaghetti sauce.

Burke carried the largest pot to the sink, where he drained the spaghetti and wondered if Lily—no, Louetta—was aware of the smile that had stolen across her face. Lord, she was beautiful. The midnight blue dress she was wearing followed her curves the way he wanted to. And she'd admitted that she wasn't wearing much underneath. Watching the steam rising from the spaghetti, he said, "I hope you know what *not* kissing you is costing me."

He caught a movement out of the corner of his eye, and saw her smile widen. Oh, she knew what *not* kissing him had done to him, all right. And she was enjoying it very, very much.

He rinsed the spaghetti and righted the pot, thinking that she wasn't the only one enjoying herself tonight. At this rate, it would be only a matter of time before she admitted—to herself and to him—that she loved him. Once that happened, Stryker would be history, and Burke would tell her about Denise, and he could lay the past to rest once and for all. Best of all, he and Louetta could get down to the business of living the rest of their lives, the way they'd planned to do two and a half years ago.

"There," Louetta said, turning a big pot upside down in the dish drainer. "I think that's the last of them."

Burke reached for the pot with one hand and deftly dried the outside, his casual stance at odds with the heavy beat of his heart. He crossed his ankles and leaned against the counter adjacent to the sink, listening intently as Louetta spun stories of how a man named Jasper Carson had founded this town with a little gold he'd found in the Black Hills in his pocket and a widow he'd won in a poker game at his side. She told him the whole tale, only how she told him anything was beyond him. *He* was having trouble stringing two thoughts together. Not that he wasn't enjoying the *one* thought that kept playing through his mind....

"Jasper Carson fathered three sons," she said. "According to local legend, they were the most ruggedly attractive men in the West."

Burke swiped at a water droplet on the inside of the deep metal pan in his hand. "The rugged look is highly over-rated."

She did a double take, and wound up smiling. "You don't say."

He shoved the pot into a low cupboard, making a lot of noise as he answered. "Any man would look masculine and moody if he only shaved once a week and spent sixteen hours a day in a hard saddle with nothing but horses and coyotes for company."

Louetta regarded him thoughtfully, wondering if he could be baiting her. There was no reproach in his eyes, but there was warmth, and a seductive gleam that reminded her of the way he'd looked when she'd taken his hand in hers and slowly licked it clean of whipped topping. Good heavens, she never would have believed she was capable of such decadent behavior. At least she'd managed to keep from kissing him, although it had required the help of the smoke alarm to manage that one. It seemed that with Burke, nothing was easy. "It's getting late," she said, thinking she'd better go home before she did something she would regret in the morning.

She already had too many regrets.

"There's still plenty of time."

That's what she was afraid of.

She hadn't realized she'd spoken out loud until she glanced up at him, and found him watching her.

"You haven't had enough of being bad, have you?" he asked.

"I never wanted to be bad."

"What did you always want to be?" he asked, uncrossing his ankles and standing up straight.

She saw his advance coming, and took a backward step. "What do you mean?"

Undeterred, he took another step toward her. "We all have dreams and aspirations. What are yours?"

Louetta swallowed. Hard. The history of South Dakota was riddled with daring adventures of gold miners, cowboys and ranchers, of gunslingers, locust plagues and droughts, but she'd always thought the true heroes were the women who'd helped their men homestead out here. Abigail Carson had been the first woman to settle in this county, but dozens of daring women had followed, some as recently as three years ago when the area bachelors had advertised for women to come to their fair town. Louetta wished she was like those women.

Doggone it. She was tired of wishing and wanting and being too shy to make her dreams come true. What did she want? Burke had asked.

"I think you know what I want," she said, folding her arms and squaring her shoulders.

He could have spouted something trite. But that wasn't his style. Instead, he held perfectly still, waiting for her to continue.

"I want some answers, and I don't want to wait until you're good and ready to give them to me."

A log popped in the fireplace behind Burke. The only other sound was the wind howling through the eaves. He knew she had a right to answers, but he didn't know what to tell her. Facing her, he finally said, "I'm not sure you're ready for the truth."

Clearly, it wasn't the response she'd been expecting. She looked at him with a lift of her eyebrows, and haughtily said, "I beg your pardon?"

She redistributed her weight to one foot, uncrossed her arms and angled him her best killing glare. "Where was I when they gave you the fortitude, the power and the *right* to decide what was best for me?"

He'd never seen her riled up. And she was right. What right did he have to decide what was best for her? Running a hand through his hair, he finally said, "All right, Lily. What do you want to know?"

"Then you'll tell me?"

He nodded. "Where do you want me to start? Ask me anything."

She took a deep breath, slowly making her way toward him. "You wouldn't believe some of the things I've imagined these past two and a half years."

Her eyes were wide open, the lipstick she'd been wearing earlier all gone. He wanted to kiss her, to wrap his arms around her and feel her arms glide around him. That wasn't all he wanted. Staring into her gray eyes, he knew that wasn't all she wanted, either. "I'm sorry I put you through that," he said, reaching out and ever so slowly taking the touch he needed.

Louetta felt herself beginning to sway toward him. The same thing had happened that long-ago April night. Then, she'd given in to the yearning that had stretched so taut between them. She wouldn't give in to it tonight. Not until she had some answers.

Moving slightly out of his reach, she said, "I couldn't believe you were really one of those users just looking for a one-night stand. Surely, I told myself, you would have come back if you were still alive. You wouldn't believe some of the horrible accidents I invented. I even imagined that you might have suffered amnesia, and had forgotten all about me. But it was none of those things, was it?"

Burke shook his head one time. "I've never forgotten, Lily."

"Still," she said, her voice so soft it was almost a whisper, "something happened to change your plans. It must have been something drastic. Would you change what happened if you could?''

The room had grown silent. Eerily, deafeningly silent. ''Are you asking me if I would change the past?'' Burke asked.

She held her ground and his gaze. ''It's not such a difficult question.''

When he failed to answer, she said, ''A simple yes or no will do.''

A pressure grew in Burke's chest, because there had been nothing simple about his decision, or about the reason he didn't return to Lily when he'd said he would. He thought about some of the things that had happened since that night he'd spent here in Jasper Gulch. He'd done the most truly *right* thing in his life after he'd returned to Seattle more than two years ago. God. How could he change that? ''There are things you don't know—''

''Just answer the question, Burke.''

He closed his eyes and said, ''To change the past would change the future. I'm only a man, Lily.''

''Is that a yes or a no?''

Although it cost him, he finally answered with a slow shake of his head. He heard her breath catch, saw her eyes close over the tears he glimpsed in their depths. He'd hurt her again, just as surely as he'd hurt her then. What should he have done? Lied?

''Lily.'' He stopped, ran a hand over his face, took a jerky step. ''I can explain.''

A knock sounded on the door. Louetta jumped and Burke swore. Recovering, he strode to the door. And came face-to-face with Wes Stryker.

''Evenin', Doc.''

Burke scowled. Stryker was all he needed. ''What are you doing here?''

The other man met his serious look with a wink that made Burke feel like biting glass. "You'll see. After all, turnabout is fair play."

Without so much as a mumbled *Pardon me,* Wes lumbered into the room. "Evenin', Lou." Over his shoulder he called, "Come on in, fellas."

Although Louetta's eyes were glazed with unshed tears, she recognized the three men who followed Wes inside. Neil, Ned and Norbert Anderson worked a good-sized spread fifteen miles west of town. They were pretty good singers, and even better guitar pickers, playing country-western music for nearly every social occasion in and around Jasper Gulch. This was the first time she'd seen their hair slicked down, a fake mustache glued over each of their upper lips.

"What's going on?" she asked Wes.

Wes nodded at Norbert, who took a harmonica from his pocket. Placing it to his lips, he blew out a mellow note. All four men hummed in harmony, and immediately broke into song, barbershop quartet style.

"Louetta is so pretty, so we're singin' this little ditty."

Wes strode to the front of the little entourage. Spreading his arms wide, he sang, "Louetta, won't you please be mine. I've been on the road forever, seen a lot of stormy weather. Now I've co-ome home to sta-ay-ay. So ditch the city slicker, and follow this guitar picker, Louetta, won't you please be mine."

A lump rose to Louetta's throat as Wes reached for her hand. "What do you say?" he asked, the other three men harmonizing in the background.

"Wes, I didn't know you could play the guitar."

"I have a lot of hidden talents. Reba's playing at the civic center in Rapid City tomorrow night. I have tickets. Wanna go?"

Louetta didn't know how Wes managed to look rugged with half of his fake mustache falling over his mouth. It reminded her of Burke's earlier statement about the rugged look being overrated. The thought of Burke sent fresh tears to her eyes. The past had nearly devastated her. And yet he'd admitted that he wouldn't change it.

"What do you say?" Wes asked, pressing his fake mustache into place.

Louetta swallowed the lump in her throat and blinked back the moisture in her eyes. Forcing her lips into a smile, she said, "I'd like that, Wes. I'd like that very much."

Out of the corner of her eye she saw Burke take a step in her direction. The next thing she knew Wes's head obliterated her view, and he kissed her on the mouth. And then he and the Anderson brothers were backing from the room, humming all the while.

It was Burke who strode to the open door, Burke who closed it just short of a slam, Burke who was the first to find his voice. "That man has a lot of nerve."

"Maybe. But I think he's sweet."

"Sweet, my eye. I'll bet he doesn't even know that you prefer folk music to country-western."

Her eyes drifted closed. When she opened them, Burke was standing directly in front of her, his face inches from hers. "How can you go out with Stryker when we both want this so much?"

Being very careful not to slide into a heap on the floor, Louetta said, "Sometimes what we want is bad for us."

"I can't believe you would consider settling for a loveless marriage to Stryker."

Any other time, his hard tone would have made her flinch. No more. Fixing her gaze on the collar of his sweater, she said, "I'm not settling for anything. I'm simply giving an old friend a chance." She turned on her heel, reached for her coat and said, "Thanks for dinner. The spaghetti was delicious."

She glanced at the back of his right hand. Without another word, she walked out the door.

Burke fought two impulses. One was to follow her. The other was to slam the door as hard as he could.

"Louetta?" he called, more loudly than he would have liked. And then quieter, huskier, "I'm sorry the evening turned out this way. I enjoyed your company tonight. And I can hardly blame Stryker for wanting the chance to enjoy it, too. I don't like it, but I don't blame him. After all, you're quite a woman. I knew it the first time I saw you. Give me a chance, too. Maybe I could burn dinner again for you sometime."

She turned slowly. The wind toyed with the ends of her wavy brown hair, but she didn't answer. Her throat convulsed on a swallow as she tried valiantly to smile. It was one of the saddest things Burke had ever seen.

He closed the door and pressed his forehead against the cool surface, thinking about the evening he'd planned. It had started out pretty well. A warm fire, hearty food, the pleasure of Louetta's company. The way she'd licked that whipped topping off his hand had taken the word *pleasure* to new heights. Things hadn't started to go downhill until after dinner, when she'd asked him for the truth. And then Stryker had shown up.

Burke strode to the fireplace, swore under his breath and kneaded the bunched muscles between his shoulder blades. The fact was, Lily was seeing someone else in less than twenty-four hours. Someone she'd known all her life. Someone who, in her own words, was ruggedly attractive. Someone she hadn't vowed *not* to kiss.

He could think of only one word for what he was feeling. It required all the willpower he possessed to keep from uttering it out loud. Louetta was going out with somebody else. And there wasn't a thing he could do about it. She might never forgive him for hurting her. There wasn't anything he could do about that, either.

His sigh was louder than the wind howling through the eaves.

She'd asked if he would change the past. His answer had been the truth. No. He wouldn't. He couldn't. But if he had his way, Louetta would forgive him.

Knowing that she was going to be laughing, joking, maybe even *kissing* another man was going to be the second-hardest thing he'd ever done. He wondered what Louetta would say if he told her what *not* returning to her two and a half years ago had cost him. Would she listen? Would it change anything?

He'd been afraid the truth would send her straight into Stryker's arms. *Not* telling her the whole truth was having the same effect on her.

Burke scrubbed a hand over his face, the whisker stubble on his jaw rasping over his palm. He'd overheard a couple of men in his waiting room placing bets on who would win "shy, plain Louetta's" hand. It seemed the men in Jasper Gulch were banking on Stryker's sexual prowess, cowboy swagger and winning boyish charm.

Burke wasn't stupid. He knew full well what a man like Stryker could offer a woman like Louetta. Hell, if he'd been a betting man, even he would put his money on the ex-rodeo champion. But this wasn't blackjack or roulette. It wasn't cards they were dealing with. It was matters of the heart. And in his heart, he believed Lily still loved him.

He had to find a way to convince her that he was worthy. And then he had to find a way to prove to her that she dared to take a second chance on him.

He'd made a phone call to Seattle before she'd arrived

tonight, and had spoken with his sister, who was coming
out here the weekend after next. When she arrived, the truth
would be out in the open for everyone to see.

That meant he had a little over a week to show Louetta
that she could trust him, and to prove to her that he was
the man for her. A little over a week.

That didn't leave him much time.

Chapter Six

Burke took a right at the corner of Custer and Maple, the sting of the north wind causing him to tuck his chin inside the collar of his black bomber jacket. Back in Seattle he'd rarely taken long walks after dark. Here in South Dakota it had become a nightly ritual. It wasn't that he wasn't tired. It was just that he had too much on his mind to sleep. Most of it centered around Louetta, and the fact that she'd been out with Stryker tonight.

Burke had considered trying to come up with a plan that would outdo Stryker's little barbershop-quartet skit. But what could he do? Hire a skywriter? Fly her to Rome?

He'd never wanted to make this a contest. He didn't want to make her feel like a prize, a trophy on his mantel, a pin on his lapel or some trinket tossed in a drawer. He wanted to see her. To talk to her. To hold her and touch her and kiss her. He sure as hell didn't want another man doing any of those things with her.

Burke crossed Maple Street, and stepped onto the sidewalk lining Main. He couldn't seem to shake the feeling that the clock was ticking. Another day had passed, and he felt no closer to a solution than he'd been last night. He had to find a way to win the trust he'd lost, and he had to do it soon. He'd been having this same conversation with himself for more than twenty-four hours—ever since Louetta had agreed to go to Rapid City with the ex-rodeo champion. He'd been thinking about her when he'd crawled between the sheets last night. Since he hadn't been able to take her to bed, he'd taken the thought of her to bed. Bad idea. The worst. He'd gotten very little sleep, and even less satisfaction. He wondered if Stryker had been able to coax another kiss out of her. He wondered if she was with Stryker right now. He'd never considered himself the jealous type, but suddenly he understood why envy had been cast in the color green.

Up ahead, he could see the rectangle of light thrown from her apartment window. His footsteps slowed as he neared. Was she there? And was she alone?

It was after midnight when Louetta wandered out to the kitchen, absently finger-combing her hair. Although Wes had tried to keep her talking, she'd sensed an underlying sadness in him tonight. She'd always suspected that there had been more to his decision to return to Jasper Gulch than a few broken bones. When she'd tried to talk about it tonight, he'd clammed up tighter than the jammed window in her storeroom. And then, out of the blue, he'd kissed her. Not slow and easy, the way she was used to, but hard, as if he was trying to prove something, to her, and to himself. Louetta had no idea what had brought it on, but she couldn't shake the feeling that it had something to do with his past. What was it with men and their secretive pasts?

She should go to bed. The regular breakfast crowd would be ready and waiting at their usual tables in less than eight hours. Pushing a heavy lock of hair out of her face, she continued to stroll through her quiet apartment, lost in thought.

A sound, like a spray of sand on glass, slowly made its way through the layers of her subconscious. She wasn't certain how many times she'd heard it, but she glanced at the window, trying to place the noise. It couldn't be sand on glass. Was it sleet, rain, hail? The weather had been mixed up for days, but the sky had been clear and full of stars when she and Wes had driven back to Jasper Gulch. A storm couldn't form that quickly, not even in South Dakota.

She strode to the window, and found herself staring blankly at her own reflection. At the sound of another scrape and *ping,* she switched off the lamp and peered down. A man dressed in black stood below, his head tipped up, a pair of black dress shoes planted on the cracked sidewalk.

Butterflies fluttered in her stomach, a strange sense of déjà vu washing over her as she raised the window and leaned out. "Burke," she called in a whisper-soft voice. "What are you doing?"

He tipped his head back farther, his eyes finding her on the shadowed sill, the street lamp on the corner washing his features in soft light. "I couldn't sleep," he said, as if that explained everything.

"I see," she said, even though she didn't.

"There's not a lot to do in Jasper Gulch."

So that was it. He was bored.

"Normally," she said quietly, "folks figure that out their first night here."

She wanted to call back the words the second they were out, because Burke had spent his first night here with her. In bed. Making love.

A cloud passed over the moon, casting his eyes in shadow. It didn't, however, completely conceal the change in his expression. Louetta thought it was very gentlemanly of him not to say anything. Fleetingly, she wished that fact didn't cause her heart to turn so soft and her thoughts to turn so hazy.

She was wearing a thick cotton shirt and black jeans. The outfit was almost as chaste as a nun's habit, but it still wasn't much protection against the cool wind. Why, then, was heat tingling in the pit of her stomach?

"How was the concert?"

The concert? Ah, the concert she and Wes had attended a few hours ago. "The music was good. And so loud my ears are still ringing. What was it the girl sitting in front of me said? Oh, yes. It really rocked."

"Did Stryker go home?"

"An hour ago. Why?"

She hadn't been prepared for the flash of Burke's white teeth. She doubted there was anything that could have prepared her for that roguish grin. He took a step closer. "I don't suppose you'd invite me up."

The tingling in the pit of her stomach radiated outward, and if she wasn't mistaken, her toes were starting to curl. Wiggling them on the soft carpet, she gave herself a mental shake and said, "You suppose right."

"It's lonely out here with just the wind and myself to talk to."

Glancing at the row of trucks parked across the street, she said, "I've heard the Crazy Horse Saloon isn't a bad place to spend a Friday night. DoraLee would probably buy you a drink in appreciation for everything you did for Boomer."

He glanced over his shoulder. Slowly bringing his gaze

back to hers, he patted the beeper clipped to his pocket. "I'm on call tonight."

It required a conscious effort to force her gaze back to his face. "How are things going between you and Doc Masey?" she asked, trying for a chatty tone of voice. "I mean, other than Boomer's accident, the pace here must be slower than you were used to back in Seattle."

"The pace *is* slower, but I like this town, although I have to admit it's going to take me a little while to get used to the constant sigh of the wind. Know what I miss, though?"

"What?" she asked, curious.

"Fast food. What I wouldn't do for a cheeseburger or a pepperoni pizza. I'm practically starving on my own cooking. See?" He gestured to the sidewalk. "I hardly throw a shadow anymore."

Louetta leaned her elbows on the windowsill. No matter what he said, he threw a very formidable shadow, the shoulders wide, the arms and torso well-defined. Still, the man was hungry. Leaning a little farther out of the window, she said, "I'm fresh out of pepperoni pizzas, but I could probably rummage up some leftovers, if you'd like."

"You'd do that for me?"

Suddenly her throat felt very thick. "I would do that for anybody."

He looked up at her long and hard, then quietly said, "How do I get in?"

She stood up, arms raised to close the window. "I'll meet you at the back door."

He was waiting in the alley by the time she'd slipped into her shoes and had hurried down the stairs. Wondering if he'd been a runner in college, she said, "That was fast."

"I'm trying to take things slow, to give you time. It isn't easy."

They stood an arm's length away from each other, her

on one side of the threshold, him on the other. She raised her eyes to his, her response analytical. Her heartbeat quickened, her face grew hot and a powerful yearning washed over her. The man was wreaking havoc with her senses, not to mention her resolve.

"May I come in, Lily?"

He softened his expression with a tilt of his head and a small smile. It was a plea for understanding if she'd ever seen one, and it cut deeply into her defenses. Pulling herself together, she led the way into the diner's kitchen, flipping on lights along the way. Tugging on the old-fashioned latch, she opened the huge refrigerator. "What would you like?"

"There's a question."

With one hand on the dish containing leftover turkey, she turned to face him.

"I'll take anything, Lily. Honestly, I'd like everything you've got."

No voice that deep, no smile that tremulous, no words that direct could possibly be as honest as he claimed to be. She wet her lips and tried not to let her voice shake as she said, "How about a turkey sandwich?"

He took the platter from her hands. "If you'd point me in the direction of the bread, I can handle the rest."

Louetta directed him to the cupboard where she stored the bread, gathering up pickles, mayo and lettuce on her way by. True to his word, Burke proved to be very adept at building a sandwich. He put it on the plate she provided, and followed her through the swinging door.

Switching on the light over the counter, she gestured to the row of high stools, which just happened to be in plain view of the street outside. "Have a seat," she said. "And be prepared for this to be all over Jasper Gulch by noon tomorrow. Maybe sooner."

"Don't worry," he said, holding the sandwich inches from his mouth. "My parents made sure my sister and I were exposed to plenty of gossip."

"You have a sister?"

He made a sound men everywhere make when they're thinking about some exasperating female relative. The simplicity and normalcy of it wrapped around her like strong arms and a secret smile.

"Her name is Jayne, and she's anything but plain, believe me."

"Are you two close?" Giving him the opportunity to chew, she rushed on. "I don't mean to pry. It's just that I was an only child, and although my mother and I were very close, families have always fascinated me. Every family unit is just so different."

He lowered the partially eaten sandwich to his plate. "My family is unusual, no doubt about that. Besides Jayne, I have two half sisters, one half brother and so many stepbrothers and sisters that I've lost count."

Now that he mentioned it, Louetta recalled that he'd been on his way to visit his half brother when he'd run out of gas along the outskirts of Jasper Gulch two and a half years ago. Suddenly curious, she asked, "You said your sister's name is Jayne. What do you call your half brother?"

"I call him a lot of things, but his name is Mason. He's a stand-up comedian."

"You're kidding."

"I never kid about my family. He and Stryker would probably hit it off. Mason spent an entire summer reciting limericks. Only, his were X-rated."

"It sounds as if you had an interesting childhood."

He made that sound again and said, "Interesting in a nightmarish way, maybe."

Suddenly Louetta felt as if she was talking to an old

friend. Leaning her elbows on the counter, she said, "Tell me more."

He pushed his plate away, running the blunt tip of one finger along the smooth edge. "Looking back, it's amazing that my parents managed to stay married long enough to have two children together. I made a vow a long time ago not to follow in their footsteps. My father has always been very good at investing his money, and terrible at relationships. He finally stopped getting married after his fourth divorce. Jayne swears she's stopping with her one. There's a standing family joke that my mother is going for the world record."

"How did you turn out so normal?"

"Then you think I'm normal?"

The warmth was back in her stomach, in her chest, in her throat. "You impress me as a normal person, yes. But then, besides having strong opinions, I guess you could say small-town people are easy to impress."

His hand stilled on the plate's edge. "Maybe the others, but not you. I think you're one of those creative types. Difficult to impress. Difficult to persuade."

"Me?" she asked incredulously.

He looked at her for several seconds before saying, "Sure you won't invite me upstairs?"

"Quite sure, actually."

"See what I mean?"

Her laughter rang out through the quiet diner, marvelous, undiluted, catching. Nothing about the conversation should have been lust arousing, yet Burke's desire for this woman had never been stronger. He wanted to ask her about her date with Stryker, but he was reluctant to remind her of any other men. He especially didn't want to break the thread that was forming between them, the anticipation that was encircling them, the awareness that was slowly, surely, drawing them closer.

"What is it?" she asked. "What are you thinking about?"

He lowered his feet to the floor and slowly stood. "Oh, I guess, among other things, I was thinking that this feels nice."

She watched his eyes closely. If he wasn't mistaken, she was beginning to trust him. Before he could do anything that would alter that trust, he said, "I should be heading back."

"All right."

"This is the part where you're supposed to tell me not to go."

She tilted her head slightly, and wavered him a woman-soft smile that went straight to his head. Before his eyes, her expression changed, and she started to laugh. "Not on your life, mister."

Feeling somehow taller, stronger, broader, he took what was left of his sandwich and retraced his footsteps to the back door, where he turned up the collar of his coat. "Oh, I almost forgot. Thanks for the midnight snack. And consider yourself *almost* kissed. Again. You could make my night, you know."

"You don't say."

His grin was slow, his gaze steady. "I like the way your mind works, but I was referring to something else."

"Oh. Well. What?"

"You could make my night by telling me that Stryker didn't kiss you goodbye earlier."

"Actually, he did."

"He did."

"But he left angry."

That was more like it. "Why was he angry?"

"I don't know. He wouldn't tell me. In fact, when I asked him about it, he changed the subject completely. Why are you smiling?" she called.

"Am I smiling?" Burke backed out the door, wondering if Lily could hear the chug of his heart. At her nod, he shrugged. He didn't like the fact that Stryker had kissed Lily goodbye, but the fact that the other man had been angry when he'd left was a good sign. "If I'm smiling, it must have something to do with you. Night, Lily."

Feeling warmed from the inside out, Louetta hugged her arms close to her body, waiting to close the door until Burke was out of sight. How many men had ambled out that door with a mumbled goodbye and a tug at the brim of their hats? Burke didn't wear a worn cowboy hat or scuffed boots, yet no man had ever looked more masculine. And no man had ever made her feel more feminine.

She turned off lights, relocked the door and quietly went up the stairs. She toed out of her shoes, slipped out of her clothes and reached into the closet for her thick white cotton nightgown. The back of her hand brushed against a sky blue satin gown she'd bought on a whim three years ago, but hadn't worn since Burke had failed to return.

As if in slow motion, she pulled the shimmery gown from its hanger, loving the swish it made as it settled over her skin. She scrubbed her face and brushed her teeth, then crawled between the sheets in her small bedroom. Men, she thought, remembering Wes's pensiveness and Burke's slow, secret smile.

Mmm...men. Hovering in that drowsy place between sleep and wakefulness, she pulled the quilt up around her neck. And she smiled.

"I must say it's nice to see you smiling, Louetta."

"My, yes," Mertyl Gentry exclaimed. "But what girl

wouldn't be full of smiles when a handsome young rodeo champion like Wesley sends her a bouquet of fresh flowers every day?''

Louetta came to with a start. Glancing around the room at the members of the Ladies Aid Society who had gathered in the diner for their usual Saturday-afternoon meeting, she caught Melody Carson's coy wink. While the other women clucked in agreement with Mertyl, Louetta gave an anxious little cough and bit her lip guiltily. She *had* laughed out loud when she'd read the card attached to the bouquet Josie had delivered a little while ago, but the smile Edith Ferguson was referring to wasn't the result of Wes's poetic apology written in limerick form. She'd been smiling like this ever since she'd found a tiny package in the kitchen. Tearing it open, she'd discovered a tape of songs by a well-known folksinger. Oh, Wes was sweet, but this particular smile had been brought on by soft-touched thoughts. Of Burke.

Some time between leaving his house Thursday following his home-cooked spaghetti dinner and talking to him in her dimly lit diner last night, things had changed between them. Or maybe it was she who was changing.

''All right, ladies,'' Isabell Pruitt insisted, tapping on her water glass and calling for order. ''I believe we've covered that topic. Now, Louetta dear, perhaps you would be so kind as to tell us how you're coming with the preparations for the annual Christmas pageant.''

Louetta cleared her throat and scrambled to her feet. ''I've chosen the music and I'm getting ready to help the children audition for the parts they'd like to play. I'm going to need volunteers to make cookies, to serve punch and to set up. Bonnie Trumble offered to organize that for me.''

''Do you think that's wise, dear? After everything we've talked about this afternoon?'' Mertyl Gentry asked.

Several of the older members of the society glanced at their hands in their laps, which caused Louetta to wonder what she'd missed while she'd been daydreaming. The meeting was adjourned a short time later, long before she'd figured out a way to ask without admitting that she hadn't been paying attention.

Within minutes, coats were donned and buttoned, purses were gathered and some of the staunchest leaders of the community left. Louetta stacked the coffee cups on a tray and carried them into the kitchen. She was elbow-deep in soapsuds when the back door opened and Burke strolled in.

He stood perfectly still for a moment, watching her. His coat was unbuttoned, his skin a dark contrast to the white shirt collar open at his throat. This was the second time he'd stopped in today, the second time he'd taken his time looking at her, the second time he'd made her heart race without saying a word.

"You aren't here to give me another driving lesson, are you?" she asked.

He shook his head, finally striding closer. "After the way you drove this morning, you don't need any more lessons. Are you having fun?"

She blew wisps of hair out of her eyes and gave a little snort. "I don't consider washing dishes fun. I swear I do it in my dreams."

"You don't say. Care to hear what I've been dreaming about?"

Burke wondered if Lily was aware of the smile that stole across her face. He wondered if she had any idea what that smile of hers was doing to him. "Are you going to sign the petition?"

She did a double take at his change in topic. "What petition?"

"The one your pointy-chinned friend insisted I sign a

few minutes ago. She said the whole town is uniting to insure that that outrageous color of green on the front of the beauty shop is changed to a more suitable hue.''

''Oh, no.'' Louetta raised a sudsy hand to her throat. So that's what the ladies had been talking about a little while ago while she'd been daydreaming. ''Did you sign it?''

Burke shook his head. ''I told her it would be unethical for me to take sides. Would you have dinner with me tonight? I promise not to cook.''

Louetta's heart felt two sizes too large for her chest, partly due to Burke's subtle humor, partly due to his innate kindness and fairness to a woman he didn't even know. ''I can't have dinner with you tonight, Burke. I have plans.''

''With Stryker?''

The bell jingled over the front door. Glancing in the direction of the sound, Louetta said, ''Actually, I'm holding auditions for the annual Christmas pageant.''

''Wow, Louetta!'' a young girl's voice called from the next room. ''You're going to decorate a Christmas tree out in the diner. Melody used to string lights, but she never—''

The door banged open, the young voice coming to a halt the instant Haley Carson realized she and Louetta weren't alone. Eyeing the close proximity of the only two adults in the room, the girl's eyes grew round and her lips shaped to two little words. ''Oh, oh.''

Burke felt his own eyebrows rise slightly. The girl looked to be eleven or twelve years old. Her hair was long and brown, an entire summer's crop of freckles fading across an impish nose and a face that was on the verge of beauty. ''You must be a Carson,'' he said, striding closer and offering the child his hand. ''I'm Dr. Kincaid.''

She looked him up and down very thoroughly before accepting his handshake. ''I know who you are,'' she said. ''How did you know my name?''

"I've met your father, your uncle and both your grand-parents. There's something about a Carson that stands out."

The girl crossed her eyes the moment Burke glanced back at Louetta. "Maybe I'll stop by later, after the audi-tions," he said. "And Haley? I saw that."

He was gone a moment later, the door swishing back and forth behind him.

"Wow," Haley declared.

Yeah, Louetta thought to herself. Deciding a change in topic might be in order, she said, "What's the matter? Don't you get enough of washing dishes after school?"

After an expressive roll of her eyes and an exaggerated grimace, the girl said, "Amy Stevenson told the whole class that I have dishpan hands. She thought she was pretty cool until she found a big, hairy spider in her desk." Haley stopped abruptly, clamping her mouth shut as if she'd said more than she'd intended.

"Haley."

"I had almost nothing to do with it. Honest."

Louetta was shaking her head before the child had fin-ished. "In that case, you'll probably get into *almost* no trouble."

Haley Carson had gotten into a *lot* of trouble when she'd first come to live with her father three years ago. Although she would probably always be headstrong, she'd lost her ragamuffin appearance, and was acquiring poise and a charming personality. But as Burke had pointed out—she was still a Carson. And at the moment she was showing an unusual interest in the toe of her shoe.

"Did you want anything special?" Louetta asked.

"Oh, yeah. Melody's out in the car with the boys. She wanted me to tell you that she'd be honored to let Slade be the baby in the Christmas pageant."

"Tell her she's doing me a huge favor."

"I will," Haley called from the door.

"Haley?"

The girl glanced over her shoulder, half in, half out of the kitchen.

"Why did you say 'Oh, oh' when you first saw Dr. Kincaid?"

Haley pulled a face. "Because Melody looked at my dad just like you were looking at the new doctor, and before folks knew it, I had two little brothers. See ya, Louetta."

The door swung shut. Moments later the outer bell jingled, signaling Haley's departure from the diner. Louetta's eyes had closed, Haley's simple observation sending a lump to her throat. Swallowing, Louetta blinked back tears and forced herself to dwell on something other than what might have been.

She placed the remaining dishes in the sink, remembering Burke's reaction when she'd told him she saw dirty dishes in her sleep. Although she hadn't said anything out loud, she used to have other dreams, too. Dreams she tried not to think about. Dreams that only made her feel sad.

She was still thinking about dreams fifteen minutes later when the door creaked open and Wes strode in. By the time Louetta had folded the wet towel and hung it to dry, he'd removed his hat and was turning it nervously in his hands. "Hi, Lou. Mind if I come in?"

"You're always welcome here, Wes. You know that."

A smile came and went across his sun-bronzed face. "After the way I stormed out of your place last night, I wasn't sure. But I guess I should have known you wouldn't hold a grudge."

Louetta found herself taking turns nodding and shaking her head. "You don't usually mosey into town two days in a row. What's on your mind, Wes?"

He was worrying his hat again. "I left in a hurry last night. I wanted to explain. I was mad, but not at you."

"You already apologized in the note Josie delivered with your latest bouquet of daisies. Apology accepted. But I'm curious. Who were you angry at?" she asked softly.

"Myself, mostly."

"Now, why would you be mad at a nice guy like yourself?"

His gaze met hers. "Hot dang, Louetta, that's just what I expected you to say. Why don't we hightail it out of here and head to the nearest justice of the peace?"

Louetta was pretty sure her brow had furrowed. "Are you serious?"

"I've been thinking about it all day. You'd make a darned good wife. You're steadfast and sensible."

"Please, you're making me blush."

He regarded her quizzically for a moment. "All these years I've thought I managed to keep from inheriting anything from my old man, other than that run-down ranch, that is. It looks like I inherited his knack for saying the wrong thing, too. But you *are* steadfast and serene, and pretty, plus, you can cook, and you're not going to change and forget to tell me. We've known each other all our lives. Dang, Louetta, you might just be the only person in this big old world who doesn't give a lick about my trophies. And another thing..."

Elbows resting on the counter, Louetta listened to the rest of Wes's spiel. He'd been very popular on the rodeo circuit. Something told her that if he decided he didn't like ranching, he could make his living as a salesman. He could be extremely charming when he wanted to be, and very beguiling. One lift of those sandy brown eyebrows of his would have most women eating out of his hand. Louetta had noticed one tiny little thing, though. He'd said nothing about love.

"Well?" he asked when the room had grown quiet. "What do you think?"

She swallowed a lump in her throat and tried to smile. "I think a lot of what you said is true. But what about love, Wes?"

"Love is overrated."

He'd spoken fast. Maybe too fast. Holding his hat perfectly still in both hands, he leveled his gaze on hers and said, "Love could come later. In the meantime, neither of us would be alone."

It was the first glimpse he'd given her of the man inside the cowboy swagger and sun-bronzed skin, and it softened her heart. It also made her realize that he was more vulnerable than most people knew.

"Well?" he prodded, the cowboy glint back in his eyes. "You gonna keep me waitin' for an answer all night?"

"Wes, I don't know what to say."

Suddenly serious again, he said, "Before you say anything, I want you to know I won't break your heart. And I'll do everything in my power to make your dreams come true."

Louetta closed her eyes, wishing he hadn't mentioned dreams. "I'll think about it. I'll let you know my answer very soon."

He smiled, kissed her once and moseyed toward the door, saying, "I guess a man can't ask for much more than that."

Watching him go, Louetta wondered how much a woman had a right to ask for.

Louetta was in a pensive mood when she climbed the stairs to her apartment later that night. For once, even a room full of rambunctious children who were filled with innocence and wonder at the thought of what Santa would bring them hadn't been able to lure her out of her gloomy mood.

Burke had stopped in after everyone else had left. While she'd listened to him regale her with stories of his unusual childhood, she'd realized that she and Burke had started their relationship in the wrong place two and a half years ago. The passion they'd shared had been intoxicating, and by far the most exciting thing she'd ever experienced, but they hadn't really known each other.

She and Wes had been friends all their lives. He wanted to marry her, although they both knew he didn't love her. Did that matter? Were women foolish to yearn to know a man all the way to his heart, to be soul mates and lovers as well as friends? Could anyone ever really know anyone that way? Burke and Wes were both good men. Yet they both had secrets they wouldn't share with her.

More confused than she'd ever been in her life, which was saying a lot, since she'd been confused plenty, she reached for her nightgown. The soft, smooth fabric slipped through her fingers, the gown landing on the closet floor. She'd bent to retrieve the gown, and her gaze trailed to a canvas poking out of a box on the floor. She glided to her knees, pulling the canvas from its hiding place. Staring at the painting of a young woman strolling through a garden filled with flowers of vibrant colors, Louetta lost all track of time.

She'd always loved art. In school it had been her favorite subject, but she hadn't really tried her hand at painting until she and her mother had gone to Oregon, where her mother had undergone treatment for cancer. At first, painting had simply been something to do to fill the lonely nights she spent alone in an unfamiliar city. But she'd discovered she had a penchant for it, and soon she was enjoying the hours when she could work on her strokes and improve her technique.

She would never forget the day she'd shown this particular painting to her mother. Even on her deathbed, Opal Graham had beamed with pride for her only daughter. "I want you to pursue what you love," she'd whispered. "You can do anything. Don't forget that."

For a time after the funeral, Louetta had carried those words in her heart. But then reality had set in, and with it the realization that the only kinds of painters folks out here needed were those who painted houses and barns and fences. That reminded her of the shade of green Bonnie Trumble had painted her beauty shop, and the petition the Ladies Aid Society was circulating to force Bonnie to cover it up. It seemed everyone was trying to cover up something. Wes. Burke. The Ladies Aid Society. Louetta didn't know what to do about any of it.

You can do anything, her mother had said.

Her gaze caught on a box of brushes and a jar of white paint she'd bought in Oregon. On a whim, she pulled the box of supplies from the back of the closet, slipped into her warm coat and hurried down the back stairs.

The wind was playing cat and mouse with a discarded wrapper in the back alley; the only other sound was that of her softly muted footsteps as she ducked around the corner and onto Main Street. During the day the downtown section of Jasper Gulch looked drab no matter what the season, but tonight the shadows took on new dimensions, the stores themselves fading to shades of gray and hues that hovered closer to black. Louetta wasn't afraid of the dark. It wasn't fear that was causing her heart to beat so hard, her breathing to be so deep. It was excitement, and the feeling that she was on the verge of discovering something very important about herself.

Trying to stay in the shadows cast by the half-moon overhead, she stopped in front of the little shop where she'd gotten her first haircut when she was four. All the buildings on Main Street were old. According to local legend, the building currently housing the library had once been an assay office in the Black Hills. It was a well-known fact that the beauty shop that was tucked between the post office and the Jasper Gulch Clothing Store had been used as a one-room schoolhouse before a newer structure had been built on Pike Street. The roof was pointed, and if she looked closely, she could see where the school bell had once hung. Bright orange curtains covered the lower half of the window, with the words Bonnie's Clip & Curl painted on the upper panes of glass.

Louetta dropped her bag to the sidewalk and sank to her knees, a vision slowly taking shape in her mind even as she reached for her largest can of white paint. She pushed up the sleeves of her coat, glanced at the moon overhead, at the streetlight on the corner. It was above freezing to-night. She only hoped it was warm enough to allow the paint to dry by morning.

She began, her strokes graceful and fluid. Before long a white trellis curved around the plain doorway, transforming the entrance, luring people inside like cool shade on a hot day. A picket fence graced one corner, and everywhere, dark green ivy trailed upward, curling around slats of wood, reaching for the sky.

Louetta worked fast, often with a brush in each hand. By the time she finished, the neon green was a lovely backdrop for fluffy white clouds and dark vines and lattice that looked real enough to touch.

Feeling breathless and alive in a way that she hadn't in a long time, she took a backward step. Glancing around to make sure no one had seen her, she gathered up her supplies and crept through the shadows, a rush of adrenaline sending her practically flying into the back alley and on up to her apartment.

Heart racing, she leaned against her door, then strode slowly down the narrow hall and into her room, where she donned her nightgown and crawled into bed.

Staring blindly at the dark ceiling, she reflected that a few things were becoming clear. She, and she alone, had the power to take charge of her life. She had some decisions to make concerning Wes and Burke, and about her life, her future. She didn't know what tomorrow was going to bring, but for the first time in a long time, she could hardly wait to find out.

"Bye, Johnny," Louetta called.

"Bye, Miz Graham."

Falling into step with the last child to leave practice, Louetta said, "You did well tonight, Haley."

Haley shrugged her narrow shoulders as if the praise was of little consequence, but Louetta recognized the glimmer of excitement in the girl's eyes. With a dramatic glance over her shoulder to check for possible listeners, Haley said, "I was okay, but I think old Isabell is gonna raise a stink about me playing Mary."

Louetta decided not to mention the fact that it was impolite to refer to one's elders as *old* anythings. Besides, Haley had a point. As soon as the ruckus surrounding the transformation of Bonnie's Clip & Curl died down, Isabell would undoubtedly raise a fuss about Louetta's decision to cast Haley in the role of Mary.

"Don't worry about Miss Pruitt, Haley. I happen to believe you're perfect for the part. Why, I wouldn't be surprised if Mary was a lot like you."

"You think she ever got in trouble for putting a spider in somebody's desk?"

Louetta fought back a yawn. "I doubt they had desks in those days, but I think Mary was very strong and very bighearted. How many girls do you know who wouldn't freak if an angel appeared to them in the middle of the night? And I thought you said you had almost nothing to do with that spider incident."

"Well...I didn't actually put it in Amy's desk, but when Mrs. Thornton cornered me in Bible school this morning and asked me if it was my idea, I couldn't lie. I don't know how she figured it out."

Louetta made an understanding sort of sound. Pearl Thornton had always had an eerie sixth sense about who did what. The boys in Louetta's class had been convinced the woman had eyes in the back of her head. But even Mrs. Thornton, with her second pair of eyes and uncanny sixth sense, hadn't figured out who was responsible for the overnight transformation of Bonnie's Clip & Curl. The incident had taken on all the drama of an old Zorro movie. Speculation had been running rampant all day, folks driving in from all corners of the county to take a look at what the Ladies Aid Society was dubbing the work of the midnight artist.

Bonnie Trumble was tickled pink with all the publicity. Even Reverend Jones had taken advantage of the "good deed," turning it into a homily that, although a trifle long, had been one of his best in years. Folks had been coming up with theories, clicking off names of potential do-gooders, only to cross them off their lists when an alibi was produced. For once, Louetta was enjoying watching from the sidelines, listening, wondering if anyone would ever figure it out. With every passing hour she was coming closer and closer to reaching a decision about what to do about the rest of her life.

A horn honked, and Haley scurried away to catch a ride with Melody. Waving to her friend, Louetta set off down the sidewalk.

The weather had done an about-face, old man winter slamming the door on the unseasonable temperatures with a vengeance folks out here recognized as the beginning of a long, hard winter. The wind *was* bitter cold, yet Louetta felt warmed. When she'd spoken to Wes on the phone earlier, he'd said she sounded different. Laughing, she'd told him she was feeling different today. She couldn't explain it, but it was as if she'd been revitalized, rejuvenated.

Wes wasn't the only man she was thinking about as she moseyed down Main Street. It made her uncomfortable. Being wanted by two men was harder than she'd thought.

On one hand, Wes was offering to share his life.

On the other hand, Burke made her feel things she hadn't felt in a long time. But he still hadn't told her the truth.

She'd had a choice to make. Along about suppertime, she'd made up her mind.

A pickup in need of a new muffler rumbled by, a much quieter vehicle pulling in to a parking space behind her. Tunes from the only jukebox in town wafted down the street each time somebody entered the Crazy Horse Saloon. She recognized each sound, but she didn't take her eyes from the mural until a deep, resonant voice said, "Hello, Lily."

Chapter Seven

Burke sucked in a ragged breath the moment Louetta glanced over her shoulder. He felt awestruck and invigorated at the same time. All because she'd graced him with her smile.

"I'm surprised to see you, Burke. According to the Jasper Gulch grapevine, you're on a house call right now."

Although he hadn't gotten used to the accuracy rate of the so-called J.G. grapevine, he nodded and strolled closer, his shoes leaving tracks in the new-fallen snow. He *had* just come from the boardinghouse where a handful of women, including Crystal Galloway, who managed the doctor's office, lived. Eighty-six-year-old Mertyl Gentry, one of the other boarders, hadn't been feeling well. It hadn't been easy to listen to Mertyl's heartbeat through three layers of clothing. He'd managed to coax her out of her house sweater, had taken her vitals, listened to her long list of symptoms and prescribed a decongestant and plenty of fluids.

"Is Mertyl going to be all right?"

"She's going to be fine. I think she likes me, although I'm not so sure about her cat."

"Daisy doesn't like anybody except Mertyl. Mertyl doesn't like many people, either, especially not men. What makes you think she likes you?"

"She clutched her cat close to her chest and grudgingly told me I have strong, capable hands."

Louetta was looking at him now, half of her face in shadow, the other half washed in pale lamplight. "I'm surprised she didn't try to pay you with a sack of apples or a roasting hen."

"Oh," Burke said, taking another step closer, "I didn't accept any payment. The conversation I overheard between the other boarders was payment enough."

"Is that a fact?"

"It seems there's a rumor circulating that you're about to make a choice. Is that true?"

Despite the surprise in her eyes, Burke felt smugly confident that Lily was going to choose him. After all, he'd seen her often these past few days, and had been delighted to discover her lightning-quick responses to the topics they'd discussed. She was coming into her own, reaching out, spreading her wings.

It had started to snow again, big, fat flakes drifting down, catching in Lily's hair, collecting on her eyelashes. Moving slightly closer, Burke shoved his hands into his pockets and studied the mural on the beauty shop. "So this is what everybody's talking about."

"Then you've heard."

"Heard? Geraldine Mackelroy came right out and asked me if I had artistic tendencies."

Louetta laughed out loud. "The people of Jasper Gulch can't stand to be in the dark. I don't remember the last time I've seen Bonnie so happy. Of course, Isabell is convinced folks should start locking their doors. It seems she's been talking to Odelia Johnson, and the two of them are certain that if the midnight artist could paint a mural like this without anybody's knowledge, a midnight bandit could rob people blind.''

Burke planted his feet a comfortable distance apart, his shoulder inches from Louetta's. "The person responsible for this was definitely light-fingered, but she was no bandit.''

"She?"

Her gray eyes looked large and luminous in the moonlight, the tip of her nose pink from the cold air, but it was her whisper-soft voice that changed the rhythm of his heart. "What time did you finish?" he asked quietly.

Her mouth opened in surprise. "How did you know it was me?"

Laying a hand on her shoulder, he turned her to face him. "Who else would have done something so beautiful, and so selflessly taken no credit?"

She didn't blush. She didn't stammer. She didn't deny. She simply smiled. A feeling of rightness settled over him, and he smiled in return. "It's time you changed your vow not to kiss me," he said, steadily lowering his face to hers.

"I need to talk to you about that.''

She never said what he expected her to say, never did what he expected her to do, but he didn't mind, not as long as she kept looking at him the way she was looking at him at that moment. "I think a conversation like that should take place somewhere more private, don't you? Come on. I'll drive you home.''

"I'm not going home.''

Her breath frosted as she spoke, her sweet, woman scent lingering in the cold air. She seemed sure of herself tonight, and daring. And beautiful. He found it hard to believe that he was the only one who saw it. But then, he had the smug satisfaction of knowing he was at least partly responsible.

"Are you trying to tell me you'd rather go back to my place?"

She glanced away, then back again. "Not exactly."

Burke felt his eyes narrow. "What *exactly* are you trying to say?"

"Even I can't believe the Jasper Gulch grapevine already got wind of this, but I *have* made a decision."

"And?"

"Er, um, that is, I'm waiting for Wes right now."

A small explosion went off inside Burke's skull.

"You have a date with Stryker?"

Sleigh bells jangled, a horse nickered and a cowboy let out a loud "Yee-haw!" Burke turned his head just as Stryker pulled a horse-drawn sleigh to a stop at the curb.

"Wes!" Louetta exclaimed. "You're early."

The other man jumped to the sidewalk, grimaced, then grinned. "I came as soon as you called."

"She called you?" Burke ground out.

"What can I say? She has good taste." The man's self-confident grin set Burke's teeth on edge. Turning his attention to Louetta, Wes said, "How long's it been since you've ridden in one of these old beauties?"

"Not since I was a little girl."

He held out his arm. "I'd say it's high time you had a little fun. Ain't it a coincidence that you called in the perfect man for the job?" With a wink, he said, "See ya, Doc."

Louetta glanced over her shoulder as Stryker whisked her away. For a moment Burke thought he saw tenderness in her gaze, but then the other man said something that drew her attention, and Burke wondered if the tenderness had been for Stryker, instead. Moments later the sleigh glided away through the new-fallen snow, Stryker's laughter ringing out through the crisp, cold air.

Burke's fingers curled into fists at his sides. He'd been certain he'd been responsible for putting the excitement in Louetta's eyes and the color on her cheeks. Could he have been wrong? The thought left a bad feeling in the pit of his stomach, a bad taste in his mouth.

A strain of twangy music wafted from the bar. Sleigh bells jingled through the quiet night. Beyond the street lamp on the corner there was darkness as far as the eye could see, a house that was far too quiet and a night that stretched ahead of him for hours on end.

Burke scowled so hard his face hurt. That wasn't all that hurt. Shoving his hands into his pockets, he headed for the darkness and his empty house on Custer Street.

Burke turned up the collar of his coat and paused as twangy music seeped through the saloon's old wooden door. He'd driven back to his house an hour ago and had tried to keep his mind occupied by catching up on his reading, his paperwork. He kept hearing those blasted sleigh bells, kept picturing Lily in the arms of another man, and had ended up pacing from one end of his house to the other.

He'd donned his coat and had set off in no particular direction. Maybe it was fitting that he'd ended up here. Fitting or not, he had no place else to go. Ignoring all the eyes that were on him, he entered the saloon and ambled to the counter where DoraLee Brown was drying glasses. "I had a feeling you'd show up tonight. What'll it be, sugar?"

He studied the row of brown bottles lined up on a shelf on the other side of the bar. "I'll take a glass of seltzer water and a little lime."

DoraLee's blue eyes held years of wisdom. Evidently she

knew when to talk, and when to leave a person alone with his thoughts. Slowly pushing a squat glass across the bar's smooth surface, she motioned for him to take a seat.

He glanced at the empty bar stools. "If you don't mind, I think I'll take this to one of the tables."

"Good idea," DoraLee answered. "There's nothing like talking to the boys to take a man's mind off his troubles."

Burke grimaced. Obviously, everybody knew that Louetta was out with Stryker tonight.

He turned slowly, every eye in the place on him. Before he'd gotten far, a man wearing a stained gray cowboy hat pushed out a chair. "Might as well join us."

"Yeah," another man said. "No sense drinkin' alone."

Burke sank onto the chair just as the man in the gray Stetson tucked a five-dollar bill into the pocket of his faded flannel shirt. Out of the corner of his eye Burke saw men at nearby tables doing the same. Rolling the glass between his thumb and pointer finger, he said, "What makes you so sure I lost?"

The song on the jukebox ended, and the room, all at once, was very quiet. A man with a thick black mustache said, "We heard Louetta was close to makin' up her mind, and we saw Wes pull up in his sleigh. If it's any consolation, I had my money on you."

"I told you she'd go for one of our own, Ben," a third man sputtered. "No offense, Doc."

It seemed no one expected Burke to answer, which was just as well, since he didn't feel like talking. With a tug at the brim of his gray cowboy hat, the first man who had spoken pushed a basket of pretzels Burke's way. "Name's Wade Wilkie. This here's my brother, Forest. Seems all the single men in the area end up at the Crazy Horse sooner or later. Beats starin' at the television all alone."

"That's right," Forest agreed. "We're all just shy but

willin' cowboys coolin' our heels in a town where the
women are friendly but few.''

"There's nothin' wrong with us, mind you.''

"That's right. Can we help it if there just aren't enough
women to go around?''

"Maybe we should put another ad in the papers.''

Talk flowed around the bar as freely as the beer, discussions about the shortage of women mingling with conversations about the price of beef, predictions of snowfall and
a new virus that was affecting the cattle in the area. Burke
didn't know much about ranching, and he'd learned a long
time ago not to attempt to predict the weather. But he didn't
want another woman, dammit. He wanted Lily.

"Did you hear that?'' somebody called.

"It sounded like sleigh bells.''

Burke's ears prickled. He'd been hearing sleigh bells in
his head for hours. These were real. Suddenly he found
himself standing at the window with a dozen other men,
looking on as a sleigh glided to a stop across the street.

"I can't see,'' someone in the back grumbled.

"Wes is gettin' down,'' a man in front said. "Now he's
reaching for Louetta's hand. He's swingin' her to the sidewalk. Now he's—well, I'll be—he's kissin' her, that's what
he's doin'.''

Burke could have done without the commentary. He
could have done without the unwelcome tension settling
over him, too. More than anything, he could have done
without the sight of another man kissing the woman he'd
been aching to kiss, the woman who'd never been far from
his mind for more than two years.

"What I wouldn't do for a kiss like that,'' Ben grumbled.

There was a long stretch of silence as, one by one, the
men wandered back to their tables. Burke stayed where he
was, clenching his teeth so hard his jaw ached. The door

opened, a blast of cold air preceding Wes Stryker into the room.

"Way to go, Wes," somebody yelled.

"Yeah, you old dog, you."

Stryker glanced around the room and slowly shook his head. "Didn't your mamas ever tell you it isn't polite to watch?"

A couple of men jabbed one another. A few of them grinned, others guffawed. "Pull up a chair," somebody called. "And tell us the whole story."

Stryker's and Burke's gazes caught, held. "I appreciate the invitation," the cowboy said, "but I think it's only fitting that I buy Doc here a drink."

Watching the other man amble closer, Burke saw no reproach in Stryker's eyes, no condescension in his attitude. He could see why a woman might find whisker stubble and a mischievous glint appealing. But so appealing that she'd choose those assets over love? That's when it dawned on him. Maybe she really did love Stryker after all.

"You and Louetta have a good time?" somebody called.

"She's a hell of a woman, that Lou."

Burke's stomach knotted.

"DoraLee?" Wes called. "Bring Dr. Kincaid here another of whatever he's drinking."

"He's drinkin' seltzer water," somebody declared.

Wes's eyebrows went up, his gaze swinging to the place where Burke had been sitting. "You on call tonight, Doc?"

When Burke shook his head, Wes sputtered, "Then bring him a shot and a beer. And bring one for me. DoraLee?" he said, as if on an afterthought. "I think you'd better make it a double."

What in the world was that racket?

Louetta stopped humming. Balancing her paintbrush on

the cardboard prop she'd been painting, she turned her head to one side, listening intently. Whatever it was, it was getting louder. She cinched the sash of her long blue robe more tightly around her waist and went to her door, thinking it was either two hound dogs howling at a treed raccoon, or an elephant had escaped from the circus and was trapped in barbed wire.

She opened her door a crack, then threw it wide. "Wes! Burke!" she exclaimed at the sight of the two men on her doorstep. "What on earth are you doing?"

The racket stopped, and both men grinned idiotically. Wobbling badly, Wes said, "Evenin', Lou."

"'er name's Lily," Burke slurred.

Louetta's hands went to her hips. "You're drunk!"

"Ya think?" Wes declared, shushing himself with one finger placed sloppily to his lips. "I might have had one beer too many, but the good doctor here's two sheets to the wind. The man can't hold his booze. One li'l drink an' he was tipsy. Three, an' he was wasted. What did you think of our ren'ition of the 'Star Spangled Banner'?"

So that's what that racket had been. Shaking her head, she reached for Burke's arm and motioned both men inside. "I think we'd better get the two of you out of the cold."

It wasn't easy to get them both through the doorway at once. No matter what Wes said, he'd had more than one beer too many. His legs weren't fully operational. Burke was worse. Planting herself between them, Louetta slipped an arm around each of their backs, encouraging them to put one foot in front of the other.

They made it to her living room just as Burke's knees gave out. "Mmm," he said on his way down to his knees on her carpet. "You smell nice. Lily? Stryker's a lucky man. An' a fine singer."

Louetta turned around slowly. "Wesley Stryker! What did you do to him?"

Even drunk, Wes had a beguiling smile. "I didn't do it, mama, I swear." He slid to the couch, his cowboy hat tipping to one side, his eyes already closing. His mumbling stopped, his head fell to one side and he started to snore.

She removed his hat, put a pillow beneath his head and covered him with a cotton throw, then proceeded to do the same for Burke. Satisfied that they would both stay warm through the night, she gathered up her brushes, replaced the lids on her jars of paint and turned out the lights, one by one.

She stood in the doorway where moonlight washed the room in a pale silver light, listening to the sounds of two men's deep, even breathing. With a shake of her head, she strode to her bedroom. "Men," she sputtered. And then more quietly, "Stupid, sweet, irascible men."

"Mornin', Lou."

Louetta spun around at her kitchen sink, her long skirt swishing around her calves. Her eyes took in Wes's red-rimmed eyes, the whisker stubble on his chin and his wrinkled clothes. Reaching into the cupboard for a mug, she filled it with black coffee. "I'm surprised to see you up and around so early," she said, handing the mug to him.

He didn't speak until after he'd taken a noisy slurp of the steaming brew. "I did more'n my share of drinkin' on the rodeo circuit, le'me tell you." Glancing over his shoulder, he added, "Guess it doesn't take me as long to recover as some people."

Following the course of Wes's gaze to the living-room carpet where Burke was stretched out cold, Louetta couldn't help wondering if Wes had intended his statement to be profound. "You didn't tell him, did you?"

Wes tried to shake his head, and ended up wincing. He gave her a guilty shrug and said, "I didn't tell him anything one way or the other. Can I help it if he assumed the little kiss I gave you last night meant what he thought it meant? Still, for a city slicker, he's not so bad."

Louetta was pretty sure her heart was leaning slightly to one side. "You, Wesley Stryker, are a very sweet man." While he was busy taking another long sip of coffee, she very carefully said, "What was her name, Wes?"

"Whose name?"

She imagined he would have been a little quicker on the draw if he hadn't been hungover. Softening her words with a small smile, she said, "The woman you were talking about a few nights ago. The woman who changed and forgot to tell you. The woman who was responsible for your decision to come home."

He jerked around, wincing all over again. "Damn, Lou. You're pretty, steadfast *and* smart." He took another swallow of coffee, reached for his coat and crammed his hat on his head. "There *was* a woman, but she's long gone, and I'd appreciate it if you didn't mention her to anybody else. A man has to have a little pride, after all."

"Speaking of pride," she called, following him to the door, "I'll understand if you want to tell folks you were the one who broke it off between us."

He turned, his eyes in the shadow of the brim of his hat. With a slow shake of his head, he said, "There's only one thing to do when a bronco bucks you off. Brush off the seat of your pants, scoop up your hat and take it like a man. If I tell them anything, it'll be the truth."

Half-wishing she could love him the way he deserved to be loved, she kissed him tenderly on the cheek. He winked, brushed his lips across hers and said, "You're a hell of a woman, Lou."

After closing the door behind Wes, she stared at the man zonked out on her living-room carpet, Wes's parting words playing through her mind. It was strange, but lately, she was beginning to feel like a hell of a woman.

Louetta didn't have to turn at the sound of the bell to know who had entered the diner. Isabell started talking before the ringing stopped.

"What on earth were you thinking?"

Placing a clear glass ball on the Christmas tree she was decorating in the diner's front window, Louetta said, "Good morning, Isabell. Would you like a cup of coffee?"

"I didn't come for coffee. Why, it's all over town. Our very own Louetta entertained two—two, mind you—men, both of whom were drunk, in her apartment, all night long. Merciful heavens, child."

Louetta glanced over her shoulder at the woman who had been her mother's dearest friend all her life. Isabell Pruitt was tall and thin. Her narrow face was deeply lined. Anyone who knew her knew for a fact that most of those lines hadn't come from laughing. She'd worn the same beige winter coat for fifteen years, the same artificial flower on the lapel for at least ten. There was a vein of goodness inside her, but it was cloaked by a fussiness that grated on most people's nerves. At the moment her knuckles were white from the death grip she had on her purse, and she was clucking and bawking like a wet hen.

"It's all right, Isabell."

"All right. All right! *All right!* Do you have any idea what allowing two men to sleep in her apartment could do to a woman's reputation?"

Louetta placed the last clear ball on the tree. "Nothing happened."

"Of course nothing happened. Nonetheless, women like us have a moral obligation to the community."

Louetta's hand stilled on the box of decorations she'd reached for. Turning slowly, she said, "Old maids like us, you mean."

Isabell gasped, her pointy chin wobbling. "Why, your dearly departed mother would turn over in her grave if she could hear you. I didn't say anything to Opal when you cut your hair, but when you started dressing differently three years ago, I told her how concerned I was. You're changing. And I'm not so sure it's for the better. Do you have anything to say for yourself?"

"Change isn't necessarily a bad thing, Isabell. You could change, too, if you wanted to."

Eyes widening in indignation, the sixty-eight-year-old spinster exclaimed, "Well, I never!"

Louetta removed a shiny glass apple from the box, thinking that perhaps *that* was Isabell's problem. Goodness gracious, she thought, chastising herself for her wayward thoughts. Her mother probably *would* turn over in her grave if she knew what Louetta was thinking. Isabell was right about one thing. Louetta *was* changing. She happened to think it was an encouraging step in the right direction, not to mention about time.

"Then it's true?" Isabell groused. "You *have* broken it off with Wesley?"

When Louetta nodded, Isabell shook her head sadly.

"I don't love him, Isabell. And he doesn't love me."

Isabell tut-tutted, but since there wasn't much more she could say, she left a short time later. Louetta continued decorating the Christmas tree, a sense of excitement mixing with contentment.

Last year had been the first year Louetta had spent Christmas without her mother. She hadn't done much celebrating. This year was going to be different. Rather than decorate a tree in her apartment where nobody else would see it, she'd decided to decorate it here in the diner for everyone to enjoy. She'd chosen the decorations carefully, some of them dating back to her childhood. Others were brand-new. She liked the effect, old melding with new. The same thing was taking place in her life right now.

As soon as she could catch a ride into Pierre, she was going to take her driving test. She was thirty-five years old, and she was finally becoming independent. Although she'd been hurt very deeply when Burke hadn't returned two and a half years ago, she knew in her heart that she had him to thank for this burgeoning sense of adventure and the feeling that she could do anything she put her mind to. No matter what Isabell said, Burke brought out the best in her. Shy, plain Louetta Graham didn't feel shy or plain when she was with Burke. She felt feminine, intelligent, animated. With him, she could be herself, a woman with aspirations. And hidden passions. Why, sometimes the way he looked at her almost made her believe she was capable of changing not only herself, but the entire world.

She didn't know what the future held for her and Burke, but she'd realized that it would be wrong to lead Wes on. That was why she'd called him last night. He was an honorable man, and he'd deserved to be the first to know that she was turning down his marriage proposal. Now all she had to do was wait for Burke to wake up, and to explain that he'd jumped to the wrong conclusion last night.

She closed her eyes in anticipation. Opening them again, she wondered how long it took a man to sleep off a hangover.

It was nearly eleven o'clock when Louetta heard Burke's footsteps on the back stairs. Fleetingly she wondered why it was that she always seemed to be elbow-deep in soapsuds when he chose to mosey into the diner.

She'd been rehearsing what she was going to say, but one look at him, haggard and obviously in a foul mood, sent her carefully planned oration right out the window. He strolled into the kitchen with a mumbled greeting and a dark look. In no frame of mind to exchange pleasantries, he pushed through the swinging door, and probably would have kept on going if she hadn't called his name softly.

He turned gingerly, as if any sudden movements might set off an explosion in his head. Once he was facing her, she dried her hands on her apron and took a tentative step closer. "What do you think of my newly decorated Christmas tree?"

His long-lashed hazel eyes darted toward the window.

"It's all right," she said, moving toward him. "You don't have to answer. I don't really want to talk about Christmas trees, anyway."

Suddenly Burke felt the way he had last night when he'd taken that first sip of whiskey—as if his throat was on fire. The whiskey had been potent and bitter, but it hadn't taken the bad taste out of his mouth or the bad feeling out of the pit of his stomach. He was a man, dammit, and had a man's fragile ego. He'd vowed to keep what was left of it intact. The sight of Lily, standing in front of the Christmas tree looking for all the world as if she was genuinely happy to see him, caused his guard to slip a notch. Hell and damnation. It nearly deserted him altogether. He had to get out of there.

"I have patients to see," he said. "And a hangover to nurse."

"Wes mentioned that you aren't accustomed to drinking."

Ah, yes. Stryker. "The next time your rodeo champion

boyfriend needs an inoculation, I have just the needle in mind.''

''I'm sure Wes didn't mean any harm.''

Her smile knotted Burke's insides. ''I should be going. Or is that your line?''

She chose not to acknowledge his sarcasm. ''You know that little kiss you witnessed between Wes and me last night?''

Burke scowled. Did she have to remind him of that kiss? Whether he blamed it on Stryker or the booze, his ramparts were in a shambles. He definitely had to get out of there.

Suddenly Lily was standing directly in front of him, her eyes soft and serene, her lips far too inviting for his peace of mind.

''It was a parting kiss among friends.''

A hundred possibilities scrambled through Burke's mind, but only one sensation took hold deep in his body. ''Friends?''

''Yes. You see, Wes isn't *my* rodeo champion or *my* boyfriend. He's just a very dear friend. I told him last night.''

The implications hit Burke square in the jaw. ''You'd better tell me if I'm jumping to conclusions, Lily,'' he rasped, ''because I think you just told me, in so many words, that you turned Stryker down. If that's so, you're free to choose me.''

She took a tentative step closer, and slowly nodded. Everything inside Burke started to swirl together, all his thoughts turned to oblivion, all his needs became one. He was out of breath, out of diversions. And Lily was out of time to turn away, out of time to lower her chin and tell him no. She didn't seem the least bit concerned. She'd had him going in a thousand directions, but all that changed when she rose on tiptoe and slowly brought her mouth to his. Their lips met, softened, opened in a kiss full of need, a kiss full of giving and taking, of passion and excitement.

His head was pounding with the mother of all headaches. It didn't matter. Need overrode discomfort. And he needed to kiss Lily, and touch her, and hear her soft murmur of pleasure.

He'd imagined the feel of her long, lean body going fluid against his, but imagery couldn't hold a candle to the jolt of excitement at the feel of the real thing. Her breasts were soft against his chest. Her waist fit his hands perfectly, the flare of her hips enticing him to explore.

Her apron bunched in his hands. Without conscious thought, he whisked it off her, sending it sailing behind her. It left one less barrier between them, but they still weren't close enough. His fingers went to the top button on her angora sweater, unfastening it with amazing ease, the back of his hand brushing the smooth skin underneath.

Louetta's head tipped back, Burke's touch sending a sweet ache all the way through her. He felt like a dream, but he was solid, hard, real. She kneaded the muscles in his back, slowly moving downward, until he moaned her name and pulled her tight to him.

Light seeped past the curtains, which were drawn, hiding them from view of the street. Her nose picked up the faint scent of his skin, a dark, musky scent that made her eyelids flutter down and her lungs draw in a deep, ragged breath. She'd responded to him like this the first time they'd met, too. And yet as she opened her eyes she felt an even deeper connection to him now, an even stronger tug on her insides.

She let out a small moan the instant his hand found her breasts. Her eyes drifted closed all over again, the sound of her blood charging through her ears mingling with the rumble of Burke's low groan.

"Oh, Burke, it's been so long."

The hold Burke had on his restraint was slipping by the second, the throbbing rhythm and crooning melody of Lily's rising passion nearly sending him over the edge. He was mildly aware of a faint jingling sound coming from a place behind him, but it was nothing compared to the cymbals crashing through his head and the explosion taking place elsewhere in his body. This was need in its purest form. This was love.

A blast of cold air hit him on the back of his neck and filtered through his clothes. And then a voice he would recognize anywhere called, "Alex, wait."

"No! Alex run. Fast."

Burke drew away from Lily and swung around just as a dark-haired waif of nearly two torpedoed himself against Burke's legs and wrapped his chubby little arms around his knees.

Burke couldn't help grinning as he swung the holy terror into his arms. "Alex, what are you doing here?"

"Me come see Daddy."

"Daddy?"

Burke turned at the sound of Lily's voice. Her face had turned white, her expression stark, her eyes large and disbelieving. The top two buttons on her sweater were open, her mouth wet from his kisses. He closed his eyes, wishing there was some way to break this to her more gently. He had thought he'd have another week before the moment of truth arrived. It seemed that moments of truth arrived when a man least expected.

"Lily," he said very quietly, "I'd like you to meet Alex Nathaniel Kincaid. My son."

Chapter Eight

His son? The dark-haired child tugging on Burke's collar was his son?

Outwardly, Louetta held perfectly still. Inwardly, her stomach pitched and the blood pulsing through her slowed to a crawl.

She saw a movement out of the corner of her eye, but she couldn't take her eyes off the child sitting so comfortably on Burke's arm. She'd never seen beige chinos so small, or dimples so beguiling. His hair was a shade lighter than Burke's, but their smiles were nearly the same.

Oh, Lord, Burke had a son.

She felt faint. Worse, she felt sick. Holding her chin high and her back straight, she absolutely, positively forbade herself to give in to either condition.

"Except for the color of his eyes," she said very quietly, "he looks very much like you."

A woman with short black hair and startling blue eyes stepped in front of Burke. "People have always said he has his mother's eyes."

Shock jabbed at Louetta. This couldn't be happening. But it was happening. She felt as if a hand had closed around her throat, and a knife had twisted in her chest. "His mother? But your eyes are blue."

The woman's eyebrows rose dramatically. "Oh. I'm not Alex's mother. I'm Jayne Kincaid, Burke's sister. You must be Lily." Casting Burke a quelling glare, she said, "I thought you said you were going to tell her."

"I was. I am."

"When?"

Burke bit back a curse. "Jayne," he said, his voice a deep rumble in his own ears, "I wasn't expecting you for another week."

She eyed Alex the way she always did, as if he were a nuclear reactor about to go off. Shaking her head, she held up both hands. "I would lay down my life for that little kid, but I can't take care of him. I know I agreed to do it until you were settled out here in this godforsaken place. It was okay as long as Ginnie was there. Now that she's gone—part of Sherm's divorce settlement along with the boat and the condo—I just can't handle that little boy on my own. I swear to God he senses my fear. Oh, no, a week alone with him and I would have been in the loony bin."

"Down, Daddy, down."

Burke's attention was riveted on Lily. Alex started to squirm. Within seconds he started to whine. It was murder on a hangover, but the hurt in Lily's expression was a lot worse. Her face was pale and her eyes looked achingly haunted.

"Where is his mother?" she asked so quietly it was difficult to hear over Alex's voice so close to his ear.

Placing Alex on the floor, Burke said, "Denise died. A little over six months ago."

While Burke watched Lily digest the information, Alex

scampered to the Christmas tree and immediately reached for a glass apple. He had the ornament broken and was heading for a table already set for the lunch crowd when Burke headed him off and scooped him back into his arms.

"No-o-o-o."

The kid was a terror on legs. God, Burke couldn't believe how much he'd missed him. Turning to Lily, he said, "He's overtired and overwrought. If I don't take him home soon, he's going to have a t-a-n-t-r-u-m. Please come with us so I can explain."

He held his breath, waiting for her answer. Staring straight ahead, she nodded once. Burke knew it was far too soon to breathe a sigh of relief.

It was only a three-block ride to Burke's house, but with Alex crying at being confined in his car seat after such a long trip and Jayne sputtering that this was why she wasn't going to have children, it seemed a lot farther to Louetta.

She'd felt dazed as she'd put a Closed sign in the diner's front door, yet she'd been aware of all the faces peering out at them through nearly every window up and down Main Street. The old-timers who gathered inside the barbershop every morning strode outdoors to get a better look. The telephone lines were going to be red-hot in a matter of seconds.

Rather than take a chance on meeting Burke's eyes in the rearview mirror, she watched houses she'd seen all her life go by through the side window, sometimes twice.

"Wait a minute," Jayne said. "Haven't I already seen that church? Burke, why are you driving in circles?"

"Because you-know-who is falling asleep."

"Why couldn't he have done that for me two hours ago? Honestly, I don't know how you do it."

Burke seemed accustomed to his sister's prattle. Louetta

was just thankful that she didn't have to try to think of anything to say.

"Your doctor's office is on Custer Street?" Jayne asked when they'd turned the corner.

"So?" Burke asked, pulling in to the driveway.

"Isn't that a bad omen? I mean, Custer died big-time, didn't he?"

Burke's and Louetta's gazes met in the mirror. As if on cue, they glanced at the innocent little boy who had fallen asleep.

A bad omen? Burke thought to himself as he cut the engine and opened his door. God, he hoped not.

Being careful not to jostle the little trouper any more than he had to, he pulled Alex from the car seat and lifted him into his arms. They probably made quite a spectacle as they trooped into the house, Jayne first, Louetta second, Burke and Alex last. Once inside, Burke glanced from the child in his arms to the woman whose face was more pale than he'd ever seen it.

"It'll only take a minute to tuck him into his crib upstairs. You won't leave, will you, Lily?"

Louetta swallowed the nerves in her throat and clutched her hands to keep them from trembling. The moment she shook her head, Burke turned on his heel and headed for the stairs.

Jayne wavered her an encouraging smile. Unfortunately, Louetta couldn't return the gesture. "I had no idea he had a crib set up upstairs."

Jayne shrugged. "Yes, it seems there's a lot he hasn't told you, but he's handled the situation a lot better than I ever could have."

"Do you mean Alex's mother's death?"

"Well. That, too. But I was referring to the situation before that, otherwise known as the little bombshell Denise dropped on Burke the moment he set foot back in Seattle a few years ago. If it's any consolation, he'd broken it off with Denise before he met you. He was as surprised as you when Denise told him she was pregnant. I don't think he ever would have married her otherwise.''

Louetta could feel the blood draining out of her face. ''Burke and Denise were married?''

Jayne pulled a face and let loose a string of cusswords the local ranchers usually reserved for use on the range. Spreading her arms in a plea for understanding, Jayne said, ''Look, Burke's a lot better at explaining things than I am.''

Louetta almost pulled a face of her own. Burke hadn't exactly done a bang-up job of explaining things so far.

He'd been married. The thought came, as unbidden as pain. On its heels came another. He'd been married, and together, he and a woman named Denise had had a child.

Burke, and someone else, had brought a beautiful, healthy, adorable child into this world. While *she'd* been crying, lost and alone, another woman had been carrying Burke's child. The words played through Louetta's mind like a litany.

All her loneliness, all her hurt and feelings of loss converged to the very center of her. Biting her lip to keep from crying, she said, ''I have to go,'' and stumbled toward the door.

''Lily, wait.''

Her hand stilled on the doorknob. ''My name is Louetta.''

''Okay, Louetta. No matter what you're feeling right now, Burke is a good man. He's never been one to take his responsibilities lightly. He did the right thing, not for himself, but for Alex. Not many men do that these days. Believe me, my ex-husband is living proof.''

Louetta turned the knob and kept walking.

"Louetta?"

Her name rang hollow through the cold winter air.

Burke heard the door close downstairs. Practically flying down the steps, he took one look at the empty living room and swore under his breath.

"What the hell did you say to her?" he snapped, startling Jayne, who was on her way inside with some of Alex's things.

"For crying out loud, Burke, you scared me half to death. I told her to give you five minutes to explain. She's out on the sidewalk, pacing."

Ignoring the choice, brotherly names Jayne called him, Burke reached for his coat. Lily hadn't left. That meant he still had a chance to make her understand.

Although Louetta didn't actually hear the door open and close, intuition told her that Burke had joined her outside. Turning slowly, she found him standing on the small porch, his dark coat open in the wind, his charcoal gray dress slacks slung low on his hips, a mock turtleneck plastered to his upper torso. He'd slept in those clothes, for heaven's sake. He had no right to look so good when she felt so miserable.

"Is he asleep?" she asked.

The tears in Lily's eyes sent a cold sense of unease to Burke's chest. Nodding, he descended the steps, stopping at the bottom. She stood a dozen feet away, the wind whipping her hair into her face and plastering her coat and skirt against her back and legs. He'd never seen her quite like this, her back ramrod straight, her lips set in a thin line, her eyes dull and lifeless. Fifteen minutes ago she'd been pliant, lithe, soft in his arms. Now she looked brittle, as if she might snap in the wind. Oh, he knew what a shock Alex's arrival, his very existence, must have been to her.

Hell, he'd been staggered when Denise had blurted it to him. But Louetta was looking at him as if she thought his soul was darkened by sins, stained by mistakes. Burke didn't know how to defend himself. He only knew he had to try.

"Lily—"

"From now on, I'd appreciate it if you would call me Louetta."

He swallowed, the sting of the wind on his face nothing compared to the sting of her quietly spoken words. "Remember when you asked me if I would change the past if I could?" he asked.

"That's hardly something a woman would be able to forget, Burke."

Her answer sliced through him like an old wound on a cold, gray day. Swallowing tightly, he said, "I answered the way I did because of Alex. I was completely speechless when Denise confronted me with the news that she was pregnant. I'd broken it off with her weeks before my trip through Jasper Gulch. And I had no intention of changing my mind. But she was carrying my child, Lil—Louetta."

"So you married her." Louetta's voice sounded as brittle as she looked.

"In the end, the fact that she'd tricked me didn't matter. I married her," he said quietly, "not because I loved her, but because I loved Alex even then. I wanted more for my child than the kind of childhood I had. More than material things and a new stepmother and father every other year. I wanted permanence, stability. Denise wasn't a bad person, and she was wonderful with Alex. I've seen you with children. They light up when you look their way. I know this comes as a shock to you, and I'm sorry. I'm sorry about everything. I don't know what else I can say, what else I can do. But I also know what you're made of. You're strong, and you have a good heart.''

Louetta wasn't certain how much more of this she would be able to stand. She felt wretched. Any other time, Burke's praise would have buoyed her self-confidence. It would have made her feel as if she could take on the world. All at once, the wind felt colder, cutting into her skin, and the world felt too big, the strain too heavy.

"Lily."

He held up one hand when she started to protest. ''No matter what you said, you'll always be Lily to me. Dammit, I'm sorry I didn't come back. Don't you understand? I couldn't, not with Denise pregnant.''

"I was pregnant, too."

Louetta felt Burke's shock, heard it in his gasp, saw it in the disbelief in his eyes. She closed her mouth, a lone tear trailing down her face. "It's true. I got pregnant the weekend you passed through town. At the time it seemed fitting, wondrous, like icing on the cake. I dreamed of the day I would tell you. By the time I was sure, I was certain you would return any day. Even when you were late, I waited. But you didn't come back. When I miscarried in my third month, I wanted to curl up and die. Alex is a beautiful child. Believe me, I know how lucky you are to have him.''

"Oh, my God, Lily. I didn't know."

"Nobody knew, except the doctor I saw in Pierre, and DoraLee, who found me crying late one night, and my mother, just before she died.''

In his mind, Burke pictured Lily, lost and hurting and alone. A heaviness centered in his chest, slowly growing into a physical pain. The door opened behind him, and Jayne's voice cut through the roaring din in his ears. "Alex is crying, Burke. He wants you. I tried to calm him down, but he won't have me. I can try again if you want me to.''

Louetta was the first to find her voice, a voice that was husky with tears. "He's your son, Burke. It's only right that you should be the one who goes to him.''

Before another tear could roll down her face, she turned and hurried toward her diner, where the lunch crowd would be gathering soon.

Head pounding, Burke stayed where he was until Louetta was out of sight. He might have stayed there forever, just him and the pain in his skull, if Jayne hadn't called his name.

He turned, finally.

"From the looks of things, that went over like a box of rocks. I'll talk to her if you want me to.''

"Thanks, Jayne, but I don't think there's anything anybody can say.'' As if his feet were made of lead, he hauled himself inside and slowly took the stairs.

"Da-a-a-ddy,'' Alex cried the moment Burke entered his son's new room.

Burke's heart turned over, landing with a thud in his stomach. "That's right, Daddy's here,'' he said, his voice unusually husky as he reached for his child. Inhaling the scent of baby shampoo and innocence, he closed his eyes. Oh, he'd missed this boy.

"Go bye-bye?''

"No, buddy,'' he said, his chin rasping over the top of Alex's fine hair as he settled the boy on his lap in the rocking chair. "Daddy's not going to leave you again.''

Alex took a shuddering breath the instant Burke set the chair in motion. He didn't know if the little slugger relaxed because he was so tired, or if he sighed and closed his eyes because he was safe and secure in his father's arms. Burke breathed deeply, the weight of his child a comfort on what had turned out to be a sad and unsettling day.

It had been a week and a half since he'd held Alex. Until this instant, he hadn't realized how much he'd missed the sight, sound and feel of his little boy. Lily had been living with the ache of her loss for more than two years. No wonder Alex's arrival, hell—his very existence—had been such a shock to her.

Ah, Lily. What did fate do to you? What did I do to you?

Denise had gotten pregnant purposely, so desperate to hold him she'd gone off the pill without telling him. But he'd used protection with Lily. For crying out loud, how many times had he preached to young patients that nothing is foolproof? And he'd been such a fool.

Alex made a mewling sound in his sleep. After several minutes, Burke carried him to the crib and gently placed him inside. He covered him with his favorite blanket, then stood at the edge of the bed, watching his son sleep.

He wondered what Lily's baby would have been—a boy or a girl. Some people would say it didn't matter, because the baby had died. It mattered to him. And it mattered to Lily. It was mind-boggling to think that he might have had another child only a month or two younger than Alex.

No wonder Lily had fainted when she'd first seen Burke at the town meeting. At the time he'd thought it had simply been a shock. Now he knew there had been nothing simple about it. Seeing him again had brought back all her pain, all her disillusionment and sadness as if it had been only yesterday.

After a long time he left Alex's room and slowly descended the stairs, his sense of guilt and sorrow sitting like a rock inside him.

*　*　*

That's it, Louetta thought, balancing the tray on her shoulder and left hand. Stay strong just a little longer.

She could do it. She had to do it.

It was nearly one. Although there were usually a few stragglers, the biggest percent of the lunch clientele came in between eleven-thirty and twelve. That meant that any time now, the crowd was going to thin out and she would be able to grope her way into the kitchen and have the cry she so desperately needed.

She'd arrived back at the diner just as the Anderson brothers, her first customers, had pulled up in their truck. Others had arrived in quick succession. Pasting on a smile, she'd swept up the pieces of the ornament Alex had broken, served up her daily specials and the homemade pies the diners expected, refilling coffee cups and doling out change to the few people who had already left. She'd held herself together pretty well, all things considered. Burke would be proud of her.

The thought of Burke sent an ache all the way through her. Telling herself to try to focus on something else, she stopped at Cletus McCully and Ben Jacobs's table. "Everything all right here?" she asked.

"Good as always," Ben answered.

Cletus nodded and tugged on one suspender, eyeing her shrewdly. "The meat loaf is tasty, but you look done in, Louetta girl. Is everythin' all right?"

"Everything's fine, Cletus." If the old man knew she was lying, thankfully he failed to mention it.

Ned Anderson, who was finishing his chicken pot pie on the other side of the room, said, "Clive Hendricks said he saw a woman with a baby pull in to town this morning. Turns out the woman is Doc Kincaid's sister. At first folks thought the baby was hers, but it seems he's Doc Kincaid's boy."

Louetta closed her eyes for the span of one heartbeat, wondering when she would learn not to be thankful too soon.

"I heard that, too. That true, Louetta?"

Louetta nodded stiffly. As usual, the Jasper Gulch grapevine was right on the money.

"Where's the boy's mother?" someone asked.

"Heard Doc's wife died a few months back."

"And the sister?"

Ben Jacobs held his hand over his coffee cup, signaling that he didn't need the refill Louetta silently offered. She would have preferred that he drink coffee, rather than furthering the group conversation circling through the diner, but it seemed that was too much to hope for.

"Odelia Johnson talked to her already. You know Odelia—"

Louetta moved on to another table.

"Went right up to her while she was unloadin' her car. That Odelia can get a person to admit stuff nobody else can, 'cept maybe Mrs. Thornton. I swear that woman has eyes in the back of her head. Anyway, Odelia says Doc's sister is getting a divorce."

"That means she's single."

"Yeah. But I hear tell she'll singe the hair in your ears if you look at her wrong."

"Is she here to help Doc Kincaid take care of the boy?"

"I dunno. Funny. Until now I didn't think of Doc Kincaid as a family man."

"Just goes to show ya never know."

"Cain't have been easy takin' care of a young 'un all by himself. No wonder he wants Louetta to marry him."

"Would you look at that sleet?" Louetta said, motioning to the window with one hand. When they failed to answer, she said, "What does everybody think of my Christmas tree?"

A few of the patrons cast halfhearted glances at the tree in the window and the sleet outside, but most of the folks were more interested in what was being said inside.

"How old's the baby?"

"Goin' on two, I think."

"Did you say two, Ben?"

"That's what Odelia said."

"And Doc's wife's only been gone for a few months?"

Louetta could practically see Norbert carrying numbers in his head.

"Louetta, that means Doc Kincaid must have been married when you were in Oregon with your mother."

"Why, that dirty dog."

"Of all the nerve..."

"Takin' advantage of shy Louetta when she was sad and far from home."

"It wasn't like that," Louetta said, her voice a careful monotone.

"Then how was it that you came to promise you'd marry Doc Kincaid, Louetta? I mean, you didn't know he was already married, did you?"

"Of course she didn't," said Marge Cooper, one of the few women in the diner. "You didn't, did you, Louetta?"

Louetta froze. A shudder went through her, the need to sink into one of the chairs almost more than she could bear. Holding on to the edge of the counter for support, she took several deep breaths, wishing with all her might that the floor would swallow her whole. The thought was fleeting. On its heels was a yearning so deep it filled her with renewed courage. Head held high, she said, "I never said I met Burke in Oregon last year."

"But I thought..."

"No," she answered quietly, "you assumed."

"Then where did you two meet?"

The crowd was made up of a dozen men and three women, all of whom were staring at her, waiting for her to answer. Willing her voice not to quiver, she said, "I met him right here in Jasper Gulch."

"How can that be?" Norbert Anderson asked. "Doc Kincaid just arrived here a week ago. And he claimed you two had already met. Why, I got the impression you'd agreed to marry him."

"Are you telling us he was here before?" Marge asked shrilly.

Louetta's eyes met those of Nick Colter, the town's new sheriff, one of the few people who knew of Burke's stay two and a half years ago. Nick shook his head, signaling that he wouldn't say anything, and she didn't have to, either. She gave Nick an appreciative smile and a small shake of her head.

Leveling her gaze on Marge Cooper's, Louetta nodded. "Burke was here before."

"How could we have missed something like that?" Forest asked.

"When?" one of the other men said at the same time.

"Even the Jasper Gulch grapevine can't be everywhere at once. Burke ran out of gas on the outskirts of town while all of you were at Grover and Pamela Sue's wedding reception."

"Let's see," mused Forest. "That's been, what? Two, three years?"

Clearing her throat quietly, Louetta said, "It was two and a half years ago, Forest." Suddenly she felt as if she'd been counting every day.

"I still don't see how you came to be engaged to him

when he was only here long enough to get a few gallon
of gas. Unless..."

For once, nobody turned at the sound of the bell jinglin
over the door. Louetta supposed everybody was too bus
watching the blush creeping up her neck an inch at a time
She knew it was only a matter of seconds before her entir
face flamed, just as she knew each and every person in th
room was putting two and two together and coming up wit
four.

"Well, I'll be..."

"I never would'a guessed."

"The girl voted most likely not to did. Don't that bea
all."

"Does Wes know about you and Doc?"

"How could he have known when none of us knew?"

"Just as I thought," an unfamiliar voice snapped fror
the doorway. "Y chromosomes with big mouths, tin
brains and a life ambition to keep the old double standar
alive and well."

All heads turned, all eyes trained on the woman near th
door, her hair windblown and her eyes flashing with indig
nation.

"Everyone?" Louetta said shakily. "I'd like you to mee
Jayne Kincaid."

"So you're Doc Kincaid's sister."

"That's right," Jayne declared, eyes narrowed. "I'n
Burke's sister, and your worst nightmare." Turning t
Louetta, she called, "Nice place." As if her expression ha
an On and Off switch, she turned her attention back to th
diners and cast them all a venomous glare. "If I wer
Louetta, I'd sue your sorry butts for slander, defamation o
character, not to mention being so two-faced it's a wonde
any of you can see straight ahead. How many of you mer
are still virgins, hmm? And if you are, how many of yo

wouldn't be if you just had the chance, to, well, you get
he picture.''

The three women in the room gasped, but the single men
yed each other warily before lowering their gazes guiltily
o their callused hands. Cletus McCully was the only person
n the room who grinned. Jayne had the audacity to wink
t Cletus, who grinned some more and winked in return.

"Louetta?" Jayne asked, rolling her eyes at how obvious
he men were about watching the swing of her hips as she
trolled closer. "Could I speak to you in private?"

"Of course." Louetta made her way toward the kitchen.

"Louetta, wait!" Neil Anderson called. "None of us
meant any harm."

"That's right," Karl Hanson insisted. "You aren't gonna
sue us, are ya?"

"No, Karl. I'm not going to sue anybody."

"Does this mean you're gonna marry Doc Kincaid?"
Ned asked.

Louetta didn't know how such a simple question could
slice her heart wide open. Staring at the ranchers and cowboys she'd known all her life, she finally said, "To tell you
he truth, I'm no longer planning to marry anybody. Not
Wes. Not Burke. Not even the man in the moon."

Begging her knees to hold her up a little longer, she led
he way into the kitchen. After the door had swished shut
behind them, she turned and faced Burke's sister.

Jayne Kincaid was a few inches shorter than Louetta's
ive-foot-seven-inch frame, but the glint in her eyes was far
oo big to contain. "It's no wonder the women have been
eaving Jasper Gulch in droves."

Something passed between their gazes, and Jayne said,
'Honey, you look as if you could use a stiff drink.''

Louetta wasn't sure what she needed anymore, but she
didn't see how a drink would help.

"Think I was too hard on them?" Jayne asked.

Louetta shook her head. "I've never seen so many m
so duly chastised so quickly."

Jayne shrugged one shoulder. "It's a gift. Did you me
what you said a few minutes ago?"

The confused look Louetta cast Jayne must ha
prompted her to be more specific, because she sai
"You're not going to marry somebody named Wes, or t
man in the moon, or Burke?"

In lieu of an answer, Louetta nodded her head. Jay
heaved a heavy sigh. "That's too bad, but since I'm hard
qualified to offer advice to the lovelorn, why don't you te
me about today's special."

Louetta did a double take. "You want to know abo
today's meat loaf?"

"Today's special is meat loaf? That's priceless. After t
tongue-lashing I gave those men, I guess the only thing th
would be even more fitting might be chopped liver. Te
me, Louetta, do you ever serve that?"

No one was more amazed than Louetta when her li
rose in a small smile.

"What?" Jayne asked when Louetta brought a big p
from the oven.

"Oh, I was just thinking that I'm glad I'm not a ma
today."

"Honey, I'm glad about that every day."

By the time Louetta had fixed Jayne a plate, she fe
better. Suddenly the fact that the girl voted most likely n
to by her graduating class had turned down Wes Stryker
marriage proposal, told everyone she wasn't going to man
Burke and set her reputation on its ear didn't seem so blea
She still had her diner, and what was left of her prid
Leaving Jayne alone to eat her hot meal, Louetta pushe
through the swinging door and entered the dining roor

thinking it was a good thing, because nobody with half a brain would want to marry her now.

Louetta dropped the phone into its cradle, nearly giving in to the urge to drop her head into her hands. That had been the third phone call she'd had since she'd closed the diner for the night. This time it had been Clive Hendricks asking her out for a drink, when everybody in the world knew she'd never had a drink in her life.

As she loaded a large stack of plates into her new dishwasher, which she'd just had installed that very afternoon, she worried that things were getting out of hand. She simply didn't know what to do about all the attention she was suddenly receiving. She had more bottles of perfume and boxes of candy than she knew what to do with. It seemed half the bachelors in town, and a few of the married men, were seeing her in a different light. There was a time when she'd hated being a wallflower and would have given anything to be noticed. This kind of attention made her uncomfortable.

In the three days since she'd let her secret out of the bag, men who had been perfect gentlemen before stared at her breasts as if she'd grown them just for them. It seemed that Burke was the only man under sixty who looked her in the eyes these days, and what she saw in *his* expression made her sad, because his eyes were darkened by guilt and clouded with regret.

She'd seen him twice since Jayne and Alex had arrived. Once in passing on the street, and once when the three Kincaids had come into the diner for supper. The conversation between her and Burke had been stilted, a kind of *How are you? Fine, and you?* dialogue that made Louetta realize what a gift the deep discussions and lightning-quick responses they used to share had been. They were both locked in their respective corners now. It seemed as if they both knew, on an instinctive level at least, that the rift in their relationship was beyond either of their reaches.

The phone rang again just as she had placed the last bowl in the dishwasher and had turned the setting to Wash. Half afraid it would be another Jasper Gent with illicit things on his mind, she picked up the receiver and cautiously said, "Hello?"

"Thank God you're there."

"Jayne? What's wrong?"

"It's Alex. Burke's on a call and Doc Masey's gone for the night. He's cranky. I'm afraid he's burning up, but I can't read the damn thermometer. He won't eat or drink, and he won't stop crying."

Assuming Jayne was referring to Alex, whose whimpers in the background reached across the phone lines and caused Louetta to hurry, she poked an arm into her coat sleeve and said, "It's okay, Jayne. Everything's going to be all right." She tried to remember everything she'd learned during all the years she'd watched other people's children. "Don't worry. I'll be right there."

Chapter Nine

Burke recognized the twenty-year-old sedan sitting in his driveway the instant his headlights flickered over it from the corner. Compared to the more modern, aerodynamic models today, the two-toned blue vehicle looked like a tank. He'd seen Lily behind the wheel of that car yesterday. What was it doing parked in his driveway this time of night? And why was every light in the house on? Something was wrong. Or had Lily come over to talk to him?

Something was wrong.

He jerked his car to a stop and got out, the flash of apprehension coursing through him intensifying with every step he took. When Jayne threw the door wide and practically ran to meet him on the sidewalk, his apprehension gave way to real fear.

"What's wrong? Is it Alex? Is he hurt? Bleeding? Where is he? Where's Lily?"

"What? Oh. No. I mean, yes, Alex was sick, but now he's fine. At least I think he is." Jayne's breath frosted in the cold air, but she sounded calm as she said, "I didn't come out here to scare the living daylights out of you. I just wanted to tell you to tiptoe, because Louetta and Alex are both sleeping.''

Burke felt the adrenaline drain out of him. It had been a long day, a long week, and he felt it in every joint and muscle. The weather had turned bitter cold, and that wind, Lord, it cut through a person's skin, straight to the bone. Tonight the wind was flinging jagged bits of snow into his eyes and down his neck.

Turning up the collar of his coat, he retrieved his medical bag from the back seat of his car and faced his sister once again. ''What do you mean, Louetta's sleeping here? Jayne, where are you going?''

''I'm taking a walk. Think I'll pay a little visit to the Crazy Horse Saloon.''

''I don't think that's a good idea. South Dakota is called the coyote state, you know.''

''Thanks for the trivia.''

''Jayne, I mean it. It's after midnight, and the only people at the Crazy Horse this time of night will be cowboys who have openly admitted that they've been too long without a woman.''

She pulled a face. ''I'll keep my pepper spray handy.''

''Jayne, at least take my car.''

''I need the exercise. Don't worry, if I can handle a selfish, greedy, ladder-climbing corporate attorney who professed to love me moments before I found lipstick on his collar, I think I can handle a couple of shy but willing Jasper Gents. Besides, the big ones don't scare me. At least they don't get fevers that soar out of sight or cry and cry and worry me half to death.''

''Oh, my God. Alex?''

''What? Oh, he had a fever, but Louetta came to the rescue. She calmed him down and eased my worries.''

Walking backward, Jayne mumbled something he didn't quite catch and started down the driveway.

"What did you say?" he called.

"Never mind. They both fell asleep a little while ago. I thought you might want to be the one to wake her."

"I owe you one."

"We're family, right? Bye, Burke. Thank Louetta for me, will you?"

Although it was freezing outside, Jayne was dressed for the cold, and since he doubted she was kidding about the pepper spray, he wasn't really worried about her safety. *He* wouldn't want to meet her in a dark alley these days, that was for sure.

Lily was another story. There wasn't much he wouldn't have given for a few minutes alone with her in the dark.

The lamp in the window looked inviting, but it was the promise that Lily was inside that drew him up the front sidewalk. The new-fallen snow muted his footsteps outside, the low drone of the television covering whatever sounds he made as he shrugged out of his coat inside. Leaving it on a peg near the door, he placed his doctor's bag on a high shelf out of Alex's reach and looked around.

There were signs of Lily's presence everywhere. Her coat was draped over an easy chair, the smell of fresh coffee reaching from the kitchen to the living room where Alex's Sippee cup had been left on a low table, along with a thermometer, a child's book and Lily's sweater.

Taking care not to make any more noise than was necessary, he walked up the steps and headed for Alex's room. He paused in the doorway, the sight of his child sound asleep in Lily's arms sending a thickness to his throat and a heaviness to his chest.

Alex's hair was fine and dark, and normally flyaway. Tonight, damp tendrils clung to his neck and forehead.

There were smudges under his eyes, bright splotches of red on his cheeks, the remnants of the fever Jayne had mentioned. Now he was sleeping peacefully, his chest rising and falling evenly.

The lamp was turned to its lowest setting, casting an amber glow over Alex's white pajamas and Lily's pale features. A shadow formed where her eyelashes rested on her cheeks. Lower, her lips were parted slightly as if she was breathing lightly through her mouth.

Yearning washed over Burke, the need to kiss her so strong it was almost a living, breathing being. He hadn't kissed her since Jayne and Alex had arrived. Hell, he'd barely seen her. Not because he hadn't wanted to, but because she'd been steering clear of him for days.

She had damn good reasons for not wanting to see him, or kiss him. There was no excuse for the need spreading through him. No excuse except that he loved her.

What good was his love, when it was his love that had made her pregnant, and had ultimately hurt her. He hadn't done it intentionally, but what good were good intentions when hearts were broken and dreams were lost?

Maybe in time...

In time, what? She would forgive him? That was just it. He hadn't known. If he had, he would have done things differently. His gaze rested on Alex, and an entirely different yearning washed over him. If he'd done things differently, would his child be stable, secure?

There was no way to know for sure, no solution, no way around this, through this. There was no way to undo it. No way to set it right. Heaving a huge sigh, he reached for Alex. Although he was careful, his fingers grazed the outer swell of Lily's breast in the process.

She came awake all at once, her eyes opening, her gaze locking on his. Her pupils were large, the irises little more than thin rings of gray, beautiful, transparent, drawing him closer, closer, until there were only inches separating them. His gaze went to her lips like the flicker of a candle, the need to kiss her growing stronger by the second.

Neither of them moved, not even to breathe. If Burke could have made a wish at that moment, he would have wished that he never had to move again, never had to break this moment in time when there was nothing else in the world except him and her in a dimly lighted room.

Silence welled around them, as if waiting for one of them to speak.

"Burke," she whispered.

"Lily," he said at the same time.

The silence came again, worse than before.

"You're back," she said in a feeble attempt to cut through the tension and the deafening quiet.

"Yes. I just got here."

"Where's Jayne?"

"She mumbled something about seeing a horse about a man."

That made Louetta smile. "She's something else, isn't she?"

He straightened slightly, taking Alex with him. "She's a lot of things. I thought I'd put Alex in his bed. I didn't mean to wake you."

Louetta came to her senses gradually, one shimmery emotion at a time. As Burke drew Alex into his arms, *her* arms felt empty. As the boy snuggled into Burke's warmth, she shivered.

She was cold. And she was empty. Perhaps colder and emptier than she'd ever been in her life. Colder and emptier, even, than she'd been when she'd faced the fact that her baby was gone, and Burke wasn't coming back.

She hadn't realized that she'd risen from the rocking

chair until she felt the edge of the crib beneath her palm. Her eyes were trained on Burke's big gentle hands as he bent over the side rails, checking Alex's forehead, covering him with a soft yellow blanket.

She breathed deeply, the faint scent of aftershave mingling with the smell of the cold winter air that had sifted into his clothes and hair. As he turned to face her, she tried to remember how terrible she'd felt when he'd left.

He's bad for me, she thought, even as he pulled her into his arms.

He's bad for me. And yet his shoulder felt so good beneath her cheek.

He's bad for me.

"I'm so sorry, Lily."

She drew away slightly, so that she could look into his eyes. She'd tried to stay angry at Burke, to blame him for her deep-seated sadness. She'd tried to remember how his leaving had hurt, how those first months without him had dragged into years. But she couldn't stay angry. And she couldn't blame him for doing the right thing.

"It wasn't your fault, Burke."

"Do you mean that?"

She took a step back, out of his arms. "Yes. I have to go."

He followed her down the stairs, hovering in the background as she gathered her coat, shoes and purse. He walked her to the door, her keys jangling when she drew them from her pocket.

"I heard you got your driver's license."

Her lips curved upward, her smile almost making it to her eyes. "I still oversteer once in a while, but I passed the test with flying colors."

"Never a doubt."

Looking up at him, Louetta wanted to thank him for his

faith in her driving skills, not to mention his faith in her as
a person, but he beat her to the quick, thanking her for
coming when Jayne had called.

"No problem," she answered. "His fever broke around
eleven. I was glad I was here. It took both of us to keep
up with him after that."

Burke nodded, and Louetta thought he looked tired.

"Alex has two settings," he said. "Full speed ahead,
and sound asleep."

Since there wasn't much she could say to that, she said
the only thing she could think of that was safe. "Burke?"

"Yes?"

Looking at her, Burke felt his heart chug to life. It was
amazing how little it took to give hope a foothold in his
chest.

"Alex is welcome to participate in the Christmas pageant
if you'd like him to. I just wanted you to know."

Just like that, what little hope he'd had was extinguished,
for although Lily didn't blame him for the choice he'd
made, she wasn't ready to open her arms or her heart to
him a second time.

"What would he have to do?"

"The little ones don't have to do anything except look
cute. He could be a donkey, or a lamb."

"I'll think about it. Is there anything else, Lily?"

He was almost sure she wanted to tell him yes, there was
something else. He was almost convinced that she wanted
to tell him she'd never stopped loving him. But as if that
particular Pandora's box was better left untouched, she
touched him, instead, the pads of three fingers grazing one
cheek.

"That's all. Good night, Burke."

In that fleeting touch, Burke sensed her forgiveness. For
once, forgiveness felt no better than blame.

He waited to close the door until after he'd watched Lily back from his driveway. She drove slowly, but she was driving just the same. Somebody had said the car had belonged to her mother. It wasn't fancy, but it looked and sounded dependable. And for Lily, it was a big step toward independence. He wished he could have been happier for her, but happiness, it seemed, was out of the question these days.

The first thing he noticed when he strolled into the quiet living room was her lavender sweater on the arm of an easy chair. He picked it up, Alex's small T-shirt falling from the soft folds. Without conscious thought, he brought both articles of clothing to his face, breathing in the scent of woman and child. He stood that way for a long time, eyes closed, one palm pressed over his face where Lily had grazed him with fingertips more gentle than a kiss.

When he'd first contemplated coming back to Jasper Gulch, he'd hoped she still loved him. He'd felt guilty even thinking about it so soon after Denise had died. But he couldn't help it. He'd never stopped thinking about Lily, and he'd never stopped loving her. He'd done his best to keep it from Denise. If she'd known, she must have understood. She'd been happy, hadn't she? He'd tried to make her happy.

He'd met Denise Parker five years ago at a hospital fund-raiser. She was a friend of one of the nurses he'd worked with. Denise knew how to dress, knew how to catch a man's eye. She was a lot like every other woman he'd dated before he'd met Lily—worldly, modern, funny and, when necessary, conniving. Denise had known what she wanted, and she'd wanted him.

It was strange, but until now he hadn't thought much about the women he'd dated before Lily. It was amazing what qualities had caught his eye then, and which were important now. Looking back, Burke realized that the biggest difference between Lily and those other women wasn't the fact that they didn't blush and had been driving for years. It wasn't even a lack of vulnerability. Denise's tears had been real when she'd confronted him with the news of her pregnancy and what she'd done. But Denise had been willing to settle for a loveless marriage. Wes Stryker had given Lily a golden opportunity to do the same thing. Yet Lily had turned down Stryker's offer.

At the time, Burke had been confident that she was about to choose him. Surely, he'd thought, once she understood his reasons for waiting so long to return she would forgive him and they would begin their lives where they'd left off two and a half years ago. Now he knew better. She didn't blame him for the choice he'd made. He understood that. But they couldn't pick up where they'd left off. It had little to do with blame or forgiveness. Instead, it had to do with hurts that couldn't be undone, and losses that couldn't be discounted.

As a doctor, Burke had seen lives saved and he'd seen lives lost. In some cases, the people left behind went through the difficult, painful process of their grieving, eventually picking up the pieces and going on. Others never got beyond the desolation of their grief. Lily was a lot stronger than folks out here realized, but she wasn't over the loss of her—their—child.

He remembered thinking she was on the verge of soaring. Now he wasn't so sure. He didn't know what to do to help her, but there wasn't much he wouldn't give to see her smile reach her eyes.

Returning Alex's shirt and Lily's sweater to the chair, he headed for the bathroom, where he stood beneath the spray of hot water for a long time. Later he crawled between the sheets, beneath layers of blankets, and stared at the dark

ceiling, listening to the sighing of the wind, the scrape o
a branch on the siding, the occasional hum Alex made i
his sleep in the next room. He heard Jayne come in at
little after two, sputtering under her breath as she passe
his room. Punching down his pillow, he closed his eyes.

There hadn't been a lot of smiling going on in this hous
tonight. Not Alex. Not Jayne. Not Lily. It seemed that h
wasn't in the mood to smile a lot these days, either.

"Come on, Louetta. It's almost over. Smile."

Louetta glanced at Melody and made a face. The Christ
mas pageant might have been almost over, but she wasn'
ready to relax just yet. Other than the slight mishap Jeremy
Everts, who was dressed as a star, had had when he'
nearly fallen off the ladder, and the fact that Melody's new
born son was in her arms instead of in the manger on the
makeshift stage, the pageant had gone quite well, all thing
considered. Haley Carson had saved the day by whispering
the lines Savannah Colter had forgotten during her brie
encounter with stage fright. It had been so endearing tha
Louetta was pretty sure that even Isabell would forgive Ha
ley for sputtering, "You're standing on my cloak, you bi
oaf," moments earlier to a red-faced Billy Andrews, who
was playing Joseph.

Louetta thought the three wise men looked very believ-
able with their heads wrapped in old flour sacks and thei
hands filled with artificial gold, frankincense and myrrh
Little Alex Kincaid had amazed everyone when he'd sa
very still, bleating out an adorable-sounding "baa-baa"
from time to time. The angels and goats, mules and shep
herds might have looked a little bored with it all, but she
was proud of the children, really she was. Still, no matte
how much Melody prodded, smiling was a chore.

Louetta waited until the last refrain of "Silent Night"—

which sounded suspiciously like "Sleeping heavy on the peas"—had been sung before she dimmed the lights. Parents clapped, babies cried, children bowed. Finally Louetta breathed a sigh of relief.

She accepted the bouquet of flowers from Josie Callahan, and was doing her best to make her smile look genuine when she noticed the lilies of the valley nestled in the tissue paper around the single long-stemmed rose. Of their own volition, her eyes found Burke in the crowd. White shirt, dark jacket, windblown hair. For a moment her breath caught, and she felt the way she had the first time she'd seen him, all soft and dreamy and full of airy hopes and possibilities.

Alex's lusty cries for his father broke the moment, Jayne's voice calling, "I'm hurrying, Alex. There, see? Your daddy's right here," carrying to Louetta's ears over the din of the crowd as everyone seemed to turn and stare at her.

Suddenly Louetta's head ached from all the noise. Her face ached from trying to smile. Her heart ached most of all. She couldn't seem to move. Luckily, Isabell took over, directing everyone to the back of the town hall, where there was punch and cookies for all.

The little actors and actresses made short work of getting out of their costumes. Soon, punch was ladled, cookies were half-eaten and the low drone of adults' voices was interspersed with the screech of children as they darted around tables and each other. By the time the line had dwindled, Louetta had recovered slightly. She even managed to smile at the parents who rushed to thank her for the part she'd played in the pageant's success.

She hadn't realized she'd stopped to catch her breath beneath the mistletoe one of the Jasper Gents had hung without her knowledge until Neil Anderson pointed it out to her and proceeded to kiss her soundly on the mouth. Her cheeks flamed. She let out a little yelp. Before she knew it, six other bachelors had lined up to do the same.

"What are you waiting for? Christmas?"

Burke waited to scowl at his sister until after he'd held a cup of punch to Alex's mouth.

"Why don't you march right over there and tell those men to back off? Unless you're enjoying the show, stake your claim, for cripe's sake."

Burke's hand tightened around Alex's cup. No matter what Jayne insinuated, he wasn't enjoying watching other men kiss Lily, even if the men in line had removed their hats like perfect gentlemen and whose kisses had been as passionate as a peck on the cheek. "They're not hurting anybody, Jayne, and the redhead on the end is blushing worse than Lily ever has."

Jayne shook her head forlornly before traipsing off to get another glass of punch. Burke stayed where he was, trying not to look on as men with a couple of days' worth of whisker stubble and years' worth of cowboy brawn stood in line to kiss the woman he loved. Unfortunately, he couldn't keep his eyes off Lily for long. She was beautiful. The way her red dress curled around her knees every time she moved and the way the overhead lights glinted off her light brown hair was impossible to ignore. The men in Jasper Gulch had finally noticed, homing in on Lily like a bull homing in on a red flag. But they were still blind. Hell, he doubted any of them really paid attention to the softness in her eyes, or the fluid way she gestured with her hands.

Burke had been certain that everyone in town would put two and two together the instant they saw the set she'd painted for the Christmas pageant. Nobody had even noticed. Except him.

Somebody jostled Burke's shoulder. He glanced to the right just as Keith Gurski and Clive Hendricks sidled up next to him.

"It's funny," Clive—a man Burke took an instant dislike to—said snidely, "but she don't look so plain anymore, does she?"

Alex shifted away from the two ranchers. Burke would have liked to do the same.

"If we woulda known she was easy," Keith sputtered, "we woulda taken a closer look a long time ago. You saw it right away. Tell me, Doc. How did you know?"

Burke's lips thinned into a straight line, his eyes narrowed, his muscles flexing beneath Alex's backside.

"That's enough, boys," Cletus McCully said, sliding a bony shoulder between Burke and the other two men.

Keith and Clive ambled away, laughing. Burke wasn't a fighting man, yet he fought the urge to follow them and take turns flattening their noses.

"Don't pay them any mind," Cletus said. "Their biggest claim to fame has always been the size of their mouths."

Training his attention on Louetta, who had put a dozen feet between her and the mistletoe, Burke said, "I shouldn't have come back here."

"Maybe. Maybe not."

Burke glanced down at the old man's craggy face. Cletus snapped one suspender and rocked back on the heels of worn cowboy boots, polished specially for tonight's festivities. "Don't take that wrong, boy. Hindsight tends to make things seem a lot clearer, but it ain't necessarily so. Maybe it's a good thing you did come back."

On the other side of the room, Louetta smiled at something Melody Carson and Lisa McCully said. Watching her, Burke could tell all the way from here that the smile didn't make it to her eyes.

Cletus made a *tut-tut-tut* sound between his clenched teeth. Shaking his head, he said, "Only things I cain't fix are broken hearts and the crack of dawn. And that woman has a broken heart."

"You think I don't know that?"

"Le'me finish. I don't know what's gone on betweenst the two of you, but somethin's put a deep sadness in Louetta's eyes. Yessirree, her heart's definitely broken."

Alex reached a hand to touch Cletus's wiry whiskers. The old man pretended to try to nibble on the boy's fingers, which elicited a giggle from Alex.

"I want to help," Burke said, picking Lily out of the crowd. "But she ducks around corners to keep from meeting me face-to-face. I don't know what to do."

"You're a doctor, and you're prob'ly accustomed to fixin' people's aches and pains. But the only person who can mend a broken heart is the person whose heart is broken. Most folks don't realize that, but it's true."

Burke unclenched his teeth, listening.

"The mending," Cletus continued, "has to come from inside a person's mind, body and spirit. It's up to Louetta to figure that out."

"What am I supposed to do in the meantime?"

Cletus pretended to snap at Alex's chubby fingers. Laughing at the boy's obvious glee, the old man said, "Exactly what you been doin'. Hug the shadows, and wait."

"Wait for what?"

"Wait until she's ready. She'll come around, I'm almost sure of it."

"How will I know?"

The old man snapped one suspender and peered around. "You'll just know, that's all."

Burke would have said something off-color, if not for Alex, and the fact that he'd had a similar conversation earier that afternoon with Lisa McCully and her husband, Wyatt, who had come into the office beaming, because they'd thought she was in labor. Burke had examined her, and told them it was a false alarm.

"Then I'm not in labor?" Lisa had asked, her brown eyes big and full of disappointment.

"You're experiencing Braxton-Hicks contractions. Believe me, you'll recognize the real thing when it happens."

"How will I know?" she'd asked.

"You'll just know," he'd answered. Now he wished he had been a little less patronizing about the whole thing. No wonder people said doctors were arrogant. Staring at the old rancher, Burke thought doctors weren't the only ones.

"Uh-oh," Cletus said, ducking behind Burke's back. "I think those Cunningham piranhas have spotted me. Cover me. I'm gonna make a run for it."

Burke must have made a growling sound deep in his throat as Cletus crept through the town hall, because Alex said, "Daddy mad?"

Staring into Alex's brown eyes, Burke softened his harsh expression with a semblance of a smile. "No, buddy, Daddy's not mad." When he happened to overhear two other men talking about Lily's new but not necessarily improved reputation, Burke added, "Frustrated, but not mad. What do you say we go home?"

Alex stared up at Burke with serious eyes. "Sanna come tonight?"

"No, buddy. Santa won't be coming tonight." Something told him he should have waited to try to explain about Santa and reindeers that fly.

"Why?"

"Because Santa only comes on Christmas Eve."

"Why?"

"Well, um…"

"Look, Addie," Gussie Cunningham exclaimed, he shrill voice capturing Alex's attention. "Wasn't that tha sweet Cletus McCully? Hurry. I think he went that way.'

The floor shook slightly as the two sixty-something-year old women streaked by, the heavy scent of their perfum lingering long after they were gone. The next time Burk looked, Cletus McCully was nowhere to be found, and Ad die and Gussie had Doc Masey cornered over by the punch bowl.

Pulling Alex's hood over half his face, Burke pushed through the door and tipped his head against the frigid De cember air.

"Whuzat?" Alex asked, pointing a mittened hand acros the street where what had sounded like sleigh bells ha jingled. "Sanna Claus?"

Burke thought he'd heard sleigh bells, too. Since he couldn't see a soul in sight, he said, "Not Santa Claus, son Just bells jingling somewhere."

Alex sighed.

Burke couldn't blame the boy for his disappointment Getting Alex, who would turn two next week, buckled int his car seat and out of the cold, Burke wondered if ther was any possibility that Cletus McCully knew what he wa talking about.

Was Burke's return to Jasper Gulch a good thing? Wha if Cletus's predictions were as unrealistic as reindeers tha flew? Whimsical, yes, and magical, certainly. But likely?

What if Lily's heart never mended?

What would he do then?

"Whuzat?"

"That's snow."

"Snow?"

"That's right. Snow."

Burke started the car, his windshield wipers dragging or

he ice crystals stuck to the glass. Driving through the quiet
streets of Jasper Gulch, he thought about the splotches of
color he'd seen on Lily's cheeks when those men had cornered her underneath the mistletoe, and the dark smudges
underneath her eyes, and the smile that never seemed to
reach them. Turning the corner, he wondered if Cletus
McCully was wrong, and if it was possible that it would
have been better if he had never returned to Jasper Gulch.

Chapter Ten

Chapter Ten

Louetta glanced up when the bell jingled over the door, the guarded wariness she usually felt these days fading the instant she laid her eyes on Lisa McCully. In her hurry to hold the door for her friend, who was struggling to get an armload of packages through the opening along with her uncustomary girth, Louetta forgot all about the sugar bowls she'd been filling at the counter.

"Lisa, should you be trying to carry all these packages in your condition?"

Before Lisa could answer, a wolf whistle sliced through the air like an arrow from the other side of the street. Lisa bundled the rest of the way inside, leaning heavily on the door. "I'm pregnant, not disabled. Besides, they're bulky but not very heavy. Isabell put me in charge of picking up the gifts the Ladies Aid Society agreed to purchase for the needy. Since the meetings are always held here, I was hoping I could store them underneath your Christmas tree."

"You know you can."

Lifting one delicately arched eyebrow, Lisa said, "By the way, who was that?"

Louetta's arms were half-full of brightly wrapped packages when she said, "Who was who?"

Lisa went perfectly still, her brown eyes delving into Louetta's gray ones. "The fourteenth president of the United States. The man on the other end of that whistle, who else?"

"Oh, that," Louetta said quietly, bending to place the packages underneath the tree.

Noise carried from the back room, where folks were gathering for the last town meeting of the year. "Yes, that," Lisa said, more quietly than before. "I'm pretty sure it wasn't a whippoorwill, and now that I'm overdue, I highly doubt it was directed at me. Thank God."

Louetta glanced up sharply.

Lisa was advancing, her gaze holding Louetta's. "It's enough to make your skin crawl, isn't it? Has it been happening a lot lately?"

Lisa's gait wasn't quite as smooth as it had been before her pregnancy had altered her center of gravity, but her eyes held as much warmth today as they had the first time Louetta had met her nearly three years ago. Mercy, had it really been nearly three years? A lot had happened in those three years. A lot had changed. Louetta had made friends, and she'd fallen in love. She'd cut her hair and changed the style of clothes she wore. She'd purchased the diner and grieved for a baby she never saw, and a mother she'd loved dearly. She'd taken up painting, and she'd learned to drive—

The bell jingled again. Clive Hendricks and Keith Gurski straggled in on their way to the meeting room, ogling all the way by.

And she'd set her reputation on its ear.

"It happens every now and then, usually when I least
expect it," Louetta said after Clive and Keith were out of
sight.

"If it's any consolation," Lisa said, "I know how you
feel."

"You do?"

Lisa's nod reminded Louetta of the way the townsfolk
had whispered behind Lisa's back, and the downright mean
things some people had said about her when they'd found
out that she'd been a runaway whose father had gone to
prison, and that she had lived on the streets a long time
ago. On the surface, Lisa had been sultry and brash. Louetta
had seen the softness right away. Today she recognized the
glimmer of remembered hurt.

It wasn't as if all the people of Jasper Gulch were mean-
spirited. Most of them weren't. Louetta reminded herself to
concentrate on those, and ignore the handful of others who
had nothing better to do than sit around passing judgment.

"Do you think we should go in?" Lisa asked, gesturing
to the back room.

"I suppose."

Picking up on Louetta's obvious reluctance, Lisa said,
"Some men whistle at anything in a skirt, but I swear it's
worse for women on the, shall we say, well-endowed side,
like you and me. Some men automatically assume women
with large breasts actually enjoy their rude catcalls and their
crude, vulgar comments and come-ons. Construction sites
used to be my worst nightmare until I discovered that the
type of men who think with their zippers sometimes lurk
in suits, too. Thank God men don't ogle me anymore."

They had reached the back room's entrance when
Louetta whispered, "How did you make them stop?"

"Marrying Wyatt helped, but if you really want to make

it stop completely," Lisa said, patting her tummy lovingly, "grow one of these."

Tears sprang to Louetta's eyes so fast she couldn't blink fast enough to ward them off. Turning her head before Lisa could see them, Louetta fought back a sob and took a sharp step to the left, only to find herself face-to-face with Burke.

For a moment everything inside her went perfectly still.

For a moment the only thing that moved on Burke's entire body was his throat convulsing on a swallow.

"Lily."

"Burke."

They both gulped audibly, and tried again.

"How have you been?" she said.

"I haven't seen you around much," he said at the same time.

She shrugged, and Burke wondered if she'd lost weight. She looked tired and uncertain, her face sad, her eyes brimming with tears he didn't understand.

"I've been keeping busy, what with Christmas just around the corner and all," she said quietly.

"A busy time of year for sure."

They were both quiet again, both uncertain.

"Lily, I—"

"Burke, I—"

"Louetta," Bonnie Trumble called from a row of chairs near the front of the room. "Isabell's looking for you, dear."

Louetta started toward the front of the room, relieved to have a destination in mind, and somewhere else to look.

"Hey, Louetta," Ben Jacobs called. "I'm savin' you a seat next to mine."

One of the other bachelors piped up and said, "Now, why would Louetta wanna sit by you when she can sit by me?"

Bits and pieces of another comment carried to Louetta's ears. She was too far away to understand the words, but the tone of voice held a meaning that was loud and clear. Lewd, derogatory, dirty.

A murmur went through the crowd, and suddenly it seemed all eyes were on her. Forbidding herself to faint, Louetta found herself studying faces of people she'd known all her life. Only a few of the bachelors wore smirks, but even the shy, sweet ones appeared to be studying the pointy toes of their cowboy boots guiltily. Lisa McCully's smile was tender, her eyes brimming with understanding. So were Melody's and DoraLee's. Burke's lips were set in a thin, grim line. Although Isabell stared straight ahead, her face wore a similar expression.

If Louetta had had the power, she would have turned to liquid and drained into a knothole in the floor, never to be seen again. She should have left well enough alone. Being a wallflower hadn't been so bad. At least when she'd worn the prim and proper starched skirts and blouses her mother used to sew for her she'd been protected from leers and jeers and harassment. She'd been safe.

From the corner of her eye she saw a man approaching. A slight turn of her head increased her trepidation and the sense of dread that was already making her nerves stand on end. Clive Hendricks had always had a mean streak, but tonight he was louder than usual, his clothes scented with beer and stale smoke so strong Louetta's stomach roiled.

"Hey, Louetta," he drawled. "You're lookin' fine tonight. Wanna take a little drive when the meeting's over? I got me a key to the motel over in Pierre. Whattaya say?"

Burke took a step toward Lily before a murmur, much louder than the last one, had gone all the way through the crowd.

"Easy," Cletus McCully and Doc Masey said, each

grasping one of his elbows. "Give 'er a chance to handle this on her own."

It wouldn't have been difficult to pull out of the grasp of two old men. But Burke stayed where he was, ready, waiting, watching.

Come on, Lily, he thought, his fingers curled into fists while blood pounded through his head. Make your move. Slap the jerk in the face. Or march over to the sideboard for a pitcher of ice water and dump it over his no-good, leering, womanizing head. Better yet, dump it down the front of his oversize belt buckle.

From the front of the room, Luke Carson called for order. "Okay, everybody," he said. "Let's all have a seat. 'Tis the season for forgiveness, after all. Clive? Why don't you and Keith help yourself to a cup of coffee and then take a seat over there?"

"Maybe we don't wanna sit down," Keith Gurski grumbled, spreading his bowed legs and stubbornly planting his scuffed boots on the floor.

"That's right," said Clive Hendricks, a stockily built man with curly brown hair and a barrel chest he showed off at every opportunity. "Come on, Louetta. Don't be offended. It ain't as if I'm suggesting something nobody else has ever suggested."

While Louetta's face paled, Clive's gaze shifted to the front of her peach-colored sweater, and then to Burke. "Guess we all have you to thank for opening our eyes, Doc. There's nothing like a startling revelation to make seeing men out of the blind, huh? No wonder you and Wes ain't gonna marry her. Why buy the cow when you can get the milk for free?"

Burke slipped out of the grasp of Cletus and Doc Masey and practically climbed over three other men in his efforts to reach Hendricks. Hell, he would have climbed over a mountain if he'd had to. Louetta beat him there.

"I've had it with you, Clive Hendricks!"

Louetta was as surprised by her outburst as anybody. She didn't know how she'd done it. She'd been telling herself to hold her head high, refusing to stoop to Clive's level, absolutely, positively forbidding herself to allow anybody to make her feel like a second-class citizen, or worse, a woman of ill repute. She remembered glancing at Isabell, whose chin was bobbing and whose mouth was open on a gasp, two bright red splotches of color on her bony cheeks. For one brief instant Louetta wished her mother was here. But then something snapped inside her, and she was side-stepping a chair and two members of the Ladies Aid Society and three of the shyer Jasper Gents. The next thing she knew, she was face-to-face with a half-drunk cowboy with bloodshot eyes and a smile that turned her stomach.

"Why, Louetta. I kinda like your feisty side." Clive grinned at Keith Gurski, his sidekick, the smirks on both their faces enough to warn Louetta that another lewd comment was coming.

Before Clive could do more than open his mouth, Louetta was jabbing her finger into his chest. "Now, you listen here. I've had all the insinuations, all the dirty comments and leers I'm gonna take from you. You grew up right here in this county, the son of decent people. If your mother and father were here, they'd be appalled."

Clive started to back up, Louetta's finger poking in perfect time to his retreating steps. "I expect better behavior from you in the future. Now, get out of my diner. And don't you come back without an apology. And you'd better mean it, you hear?"

"For cryin' out loud, Clive," Keith Gurski bellowed

from a dozen feet away. "You gonna take that from a gal like her?"

Keith never saw the right hook coming, but the crack of Burke's fist as it made contact with Keith's bony jaw echoed throughout the entire room.

"Jumpin' Jennifer!" the other man yelled hoarsely, holding on to his jaw. "It's a little late to be defending Louetta's honor. You're the one who saw your chance a few years back and took it."

Cradling his right hand in his left one, Burke spun around. "It wasn't like that!"

"Yeah? Well, why don't you tell us all how it was!"

Odelia Johnson, the town gossip second only to Isabell Pruitt, jumped to her feet so fast her chair scraped backward. Clutching one hand over her ample bosom, Odelia exclaimed, "Why, this is scandalous, that's what this is. It's bad enough that our very own Clive and Keith came here reeking of spirits and speaking such vulgarities to our shy, sweet Louetta. Why, the poor child's reputation is ruined. And it's as much Dr. Kincaid's fault as anybody's. I think we ladies of the society should consider boycotting his practice, and another thing—"

"Odelia!" Isabell cut in. "You've been like a sister to me all my life, but there's a reason God gave everyone two ears and only one mouth. It's so we can listen twice as much as we talk."

While a dumbfounded Odelia sank into her chair, one of the Jasper Gents mumbled, "If that ain't the pot callin' the kettle black, I don't know what is."

Head held high, Isabell ignored the quip and nodded for Burke to continue. Burke could have kissed the old maid. But first, he had something far more important to do.

He strode to the front of the room, nodded at the Carson brothers, who had given up all pretense of attempting to call for order, and cast an all-encompassing glance at the men in the room. "What I saw two and a half years ago was a woman with beautiful eyes and a smile soft enough to warm a man despite the South Dakota wind. You've had thirty-five years to recognize her beauty, and yet you've never seen the writing on the wall. Or should I say the painting."

Cowboy hats were pushed high on foreheads. "Painting?"

Mouths opened on gasps. "Do you mean—"

"That's right," Burke said. "Your very own Louetta Graham painted that mural on Bonnie's shop. She has artist's hands. I can't believe none of you ever noticed."

"Why, Louetta," Bonnie gasped. "You did that for me?"

Louetta's voice quivered. "I wanted to help, Bonnie."

Burke's gaze found her in the crowd. Suddenly his throat felt thick, his heart chugged to life and the throbbing pain in his right hand all but disappeared. She was looking at him, one finger still suspended in midair following that last jab she'd given Clive's chest. Her eyes looked large from here, her hair waving in disarray to her shoulders. This was no sparrow perched on the edge of her nest, trying to get up her courage to take to the air. This was an eagle, already soaring.

"I hurt you," he said, his voice quieter than before. "I'd do anything to be able to undo that. But no matter what anybody says, you were never just a chance I saw and took. I fell in love with you the first night we met. And I'll gladly take on every man in town if I have to."

He squared his shoulders and raised his chin, eyes narrowing as he cast an ominous glare around the room. "I'm not giving up, and if anybody wants to sully Lily's reputation, he'll have to answer to me."

"Who's Lily?"

"Louetta, you idiot."

"Why didn't he say so?"

"Shh."

"You shush."

More voices were raised. Louetta barely heard. All her attention was trained on Burke. Dark slacks, white shirt, windblown hair.

"Say that again." Her voice sounded breathless and a little wobbly, but it was loud enough to carry to the center of the room where Burke stood.

Before her eyes, his throat convulsed on a swallow. "They had thirty-five years to recognize your beauty."

She shook her head, steadily moving closer. "Not that part."

"I'll take on every man in town if I have to."

Again she shook her head. "I can take on the men myself." And then, feeling bold, brave, reborn, she said, "All right. You can help if you want to."

A seductive heat came into his eyes. "I guess you're going to have to tell me what it is you want me to repeat."

The challenge came through loud and clear. Stopping a few feet away from him, she said, "Is that a fact?"

If Burke lived to be a hundred, he would never forget the way she looked at that moment, her eyes artful and serene, her lips shaped to a smile that stole his breath away.

"You really fell in love with me that night?"

At his nod, her smile widened. "But of course you did."

Happiness took root in his chest, spreading lower in a way that made him very happy to be alive. He had every intention of sweeping her into his arms and carrying her to some quiet place. But first, there was something else he'd been waiting two and a half years to do.

He took the few remaining steps separating them and

sank to one knee the way Wes Stryker had at the town meeting a month ago. Reaching for her hand, as slender and graceful as any artist's he'd ever seen, Burke said, ' know this isn't the first marriage proposal you've received but it's the first one I've made. Will you marry me, Lily Will you be my wife, my partner, my soul mate?''

Tears gathered in Louetta's eyes, spilling over her lashes trailing down her smooth, pale cheeks. She smiled the most beautiful smile the folks of Jasper Gulch had ever seen Behind them, Isabell Pruitt sniffled into a handkerchief an the area bachelors shuffled in their chairs.

"Well, I'll be."

"Blind. That's what we've been."

"And stupid."

"Our very own Louetta was the midnight artist."

"And we let her get away."

Clive and Keith slunk shamefacedly out the back door

"Well?" Burke asked when the cold air blasting into the room rustled his collar and fluttered a lock of Lily's wavy hair. "Will you marry me?"

Louetta nodded, and a cheer rang from the crowd.

"When?" he asked, slowly rising to his feet.

Louetta's gaze followed him up, her heart brimming with so much love and happiness she couldn't contain it all "I've always dreamed of a Christmas wedding."

A slow heat burned in his eyes. "This Christmas? O next?"

She reached her hand up, gently laying her palm on his lean cheek. "Oh," the people closest to them heard her say, "I don't think I could wait until next Christmas."

The Anderson brothers grudgingly said, "Looks like we'll be playing the music for another weddin' reception."

Without taking his eyes from Lily, Burke said, "You boys ever play folk music?"

Cletus McCully snapped one suspender. Doc Masey took a handkerchief from his pocket and cleaned his glasses just as Lisa McCully groaned out loud.

"Sorry for the interruption," she said when all eyes turned to her. "But that one practically cut me in half."

"You're in labor?" Burke asked incredulously.

She nodded. "You were right. When it's the real thing, a person just knows."

Burke and Louetta shared a meaningful look.

"Goodness gracious," Isabell Pruitt exclaimed, rising to her feet.

"Another new baby is about to be born here in Jasper Gulch," Bonnie Trumble added proudly.

"Luke, Clayton," Isabell sputtered. "You must postpone the meeting immediately."

The meeting was postponed.

"Where's that sweet husband of yours?" Odelia Johnson asked Lisa.

"Wyatt's at a police training session in Pierre." Another pain sent her sinking into a chair. "Oh, my."

"Don't just stand there, doctors," Isabell bossed. "Get this woman to the hospital."

"I'm getting old," Doc Masey said. "I think I'll sit this one out. Burke?"

"I'll get my bag," Burke said.

"I'll drive," Louetta declared.

Everyone stopped to stare, but for a moment Burke and Louetta had eyes only for each other. The noise in the room reached a deafening roar as chairs were scraped against the floor, orders were barked, bachelors shuffled their feet in their haste to get out of there and into the Crazy Horse to nurse their egos and call themselves fools to let Louetta Graham get away.

Isabell and Odelia helped Lisa from the room. "Doct
please!" Isabell sputtered.

"It's all right," Lisa said. "Burke and Louetta have bee
waiting a long time for this moment. Little Rose here ca
wait a minute or two until they're through. Let's give the
a moment to themselves."

The room emptied, leaving Burke and Lily alone. The
were so many things Louetta wanted to say, and yet th
only thing she could think of at that moment was, "Lis
and Wyatt are going to name their baby Rose?"

Burke nodded one time. "I reserved the name Lily fo
our first daughter."

"Oh, Burke."

Their gazes were trained on each other, their faces draw
ing closer, eyelashes dropping, lips seeking. Their kiss wa
just a brush of air at first, slowly growing more intimat
enhanced as much by the time they'd been apart as by he
gentle sway toward him, and his deep sigh. The kis
brought more than a rush of blood and a flutter of hear
beats, for in that kiss, mended hearts were joined, an
promises were kept.

"After little Rose is born," Louetta whispered close t
Burke's ear, "I'd like to go see Alex."

Emotion filled Burke's chest, thickened his throat an
sent renewed need to the very center of him.

"What?" she whispered, as mesmerized by the heat i
his eyes as he was by the heat in hers.

"I was just thinking how glad I am that I ran out of ga
in a little town called Jasper Gulch."

For a moment they both imagined how their lives woul
have been if that had never happened. Burke never woul
have known real love. And Louetta never would hav
known Burke.

"Lisa was right about how long I've waited for this,"

⸱ said. "I don't know how I'm going to wait another
week."

"Ahem," Isabell said from the doorway.

Louetta's smile was artful and serene. "All in good time,
Burke. After all, we're living proof that good things happen
to those who wait."

Without another word, they hurried, hand in hand, out
into the cold December air.

Candles flickered inside the little white church on the
corner, casting a golden glow over Louetta's long ivory
gown and Burke's crisp white shirt. So far, the ceremony
had been short and poignant, little Rose McCully's lusty
cries and subsequent suckling somehow adding to the rich-
ness of the day. Red poinsettias lined the deep windowsills,
pine boughs circling the pillars, red bows decorating the
ends of every pew.

No one minded the fact that Alex had witnessed his father's marriage perched on Burke's arm. After all, who
could blame the boy? He was as mesmerized by the light
in Louetta's eyes as everyone else was.

"Who would have thought," Edith Ferguson whispered,
"that our very own Louetta would become a doctor's
wife?"

The voices of Doc Masey and Isabell Pruitt came in uni-
son. "Why, I knew it all along."

Doc's eyebrows went up. Isabell blushed to the roots of
her springy gray hair. Cletus McCully's quiet laughter
blended with the ringing of church bells and sleigh bells
and the hiss of Odelia Johnson's voice as she said, "Shh."

Moments later Reverend Jones said, "Do you, Burke
Kincaid, take our very own Louetta Graham to be your
lawfully wedded wife?"

Tears brimmed in Louetta's eyes as Burke answered, do.''

As usual, Cletus paid little heed to those clucking hens of the Ladies Aid Society. Nudging Wes Stryker, who was sitting next to him, Cletus whispered, ''Don't take it to heart, boy. More women will come to Jasper Gulch. You'll see....''

''Do you, Louetta Graham,'' Reverend Jones asked, ''take this man to be your lawfully wedded husband?''

''I do,'' she said so softly folks had to strain to hear.

''Wes?'' Cletus whispered.

Wes didn't move, not to answer, not even to breathe. Following the course of Wes's gaze, Cletus hooked a thumb through one suspender and started to grin. Good ole Wes didn't appear to be pining away after Louetta after all. Why, he was looking at Doc Kincaid's sister.

''Here we go again,'' Cletus said under his breath, Doc Masey and Isabell on his left, Wes on his right.

''Yee-haw. Here we go again.''

*   *   *   *   *

Yep, you guessed it, Wes Stryker's story is next.
Sandra Steffen's immensely popular
BACHELOR GULCH series
will continue in 1999,
only in Silhouette Romance!

SOMETIMES THE SMALLEST PACKAGES CAN LEAD TO THE BIGGEST SURPRISES!

February 1999
A VOW, A RING, A BABY SWING
by Teresa Southwick (SR #1349)

Pregnant and alone, Rosie Marchetti had just been stood up at the altar. So family friend Steve Schafer stepped up the aisle and married her. Now Rosie is trying to convince him that this family was meant to be....

May 1999
THE BABY ARRANGEMENT
by Moyra Tarling (SR #1368)

Jared McAndrew has been searching for his son, and when he discovers Faith Nelson with his child he demands she come home with him. Can Faith convince Jared that he has the wrong mother—but the right bride?

Enjoy these stories of love and family. And look for future BUNDLES OF JOY titles from Leanna Wilson and Suzanne McMinn coming in the fall of 1999.

BUNDLES OF JOY
only from

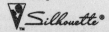

Available wherever Silhouette books are sold.

Take 2 bestselling love stories FREE

Plus get a FREE surprise gift!

Special Limited-Time Offer

Mail to Silhouette Reader Service™

3010 Walden Avenue
P.O. Box 1867
Buffalo, N.Y. 14240-1867

YES! Please send me 2 free Silhouette Romance™ novels and my free surprise gift. Then send me 6 brand-new novels every month, which I will receive months before they appear in bookstores. Bill me at the low price of $2.90 each plus 25¢ delivery and applicable sales tax, if any.* That's the complete price, and a saving of over 10% off the cover prices—quite a bargain! I understand that accepting the books and gift places me under no obligation ever to buy any books. I can always return a shipment and cancel at any time. Even if I never buy another book from Silhouette, the 2 free books and the surprise gift are mine to keep forever.

215 SEN CH7S

Name	(PLEASE PRINT)	
Address	Apt. No.	
City	State	Zip

This offer is limited to one order per household and not valid to present Silhouette Romance™ subscribers. *Terms and prices are subject to change without notice. Sales tax applicable in N.Y.

USROM-98   ©1990 Harlequin Enterprises Limited

Beloved author *Judy Christenberry*
brings us an exciting new miniseries in

LUCKY CHARM SISTERS

Meet Kate in January 1999 in
MARRY ME, KATE (SR #1344)
He needed to avoid others meddling in his life. *She*
needed money to rebuild her father's dream. So William
Hardison and Kate O'Connor struck a bargain....

Join Maggie in February 1999 in
BABY IN HER ARMS (SR #1350)
Once Josh McKinney found his infant girl, he needed a
baby expert—quickly! But the more time Josh spent with
her, the more he wanted to make Maggie O'Connor his
real wife....

Don't miss Susan in March 1999 in
A RING FOR CINDERELLA (SR #1356)
The last thing Susan Greenwood expected was a marriage proposal! But cowboy Zack Lowery needed a
fiancée to fulfill his grandfather's dying wish....

A boss, a brain and a beauty. Three sisters marry for
convenience...but will they find love?

THE LUCKY CHARM SISTERS only from

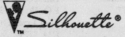

Available wherever Silhouette books are sold.

For a limited time, Harlequin and Silhouette have an offer you just can't refuse.

In November and December 1998:

BUY **ANY** TWO HARLEQUIN
OR SILHOUETTE BOOKS and
SAVE $10.00
off future purchases

OR BUY ANY THREE HARLEQUIN OR SILHOUETTE BOOKS
AND **SAVE $20.00** OFF FUTURE PURCHASES!

(each coupon is good for $1.00 off the purchase of two
Harlequin or Silhouette books)

....

JUST BUY 2 HARLEQUIN OR SILHOUETTE BOOKS, SEND US YOUR
NAME, ADDRESS AND 2 PROOFS OF PURCHASE (CASH REGISTER
RECEIPTS) AND HARLEQUIN WILL SEND YOU A COUPON BOOKLET
WORTH $10.00 OFF FUTURE PURCHASES OF HARLEQUIN OR
SILHOUETTE BOOKS IN 1999. SEND US 3 PROOFS OF PURCHASE AND
WE WILL SEND YOU 2 COUPON BOOKLETS WITH A TOTAL SAVING OF
$20.00. (ALLOW 4-6 WEEKS DELIVERY) OFFER EXPIRES
DECEMBER 31, 1998.

....

I accept your offer! Please send me a coupon booklet(s), to:

NAME: _____

ADDRESS: _____

CITY: _____ STATE/PROV.: _____ POSTAL/ZIP CODE: _____

Send your name and address, along with your cash register
receipts for proofs of purchase, to:

In the U.S.	In Canada
Harlequin Books	**Harlequin Books**
P.O. Box 9057	**P.O. Box 622**
Buffalo, NY	**Fort Erie, Ontario**
14269	**L2A 5X3**

Bestselling author

LINDSAY McKENNA

continues the drama and adventure of her
popular series with an all-new, longer-length
single-title romance:

MORGAN'S MERCENARIES

HEART OF THE JAGUAR

Major Mike Houston and Dr. Ann Parsons were in the heat
of the jungle, deep in enemy territory. She knew Mike's
warrior blood kept him from the life—and the love—he
silently craved. And now she had so much more at stake.
For the beautiful doctor carried a child. His child...

Available in January 1999, at your favorite retail outlet!

Look for more **MORGAN'S MERCENARIES** in 1999,
as the excitement continues in the Special Edition line!

Silhouette®

PSMORGMERC

Silhouette ROMANCE™

COMING NEXT MONTH

#1342 THE BOSS AND THE BEAUTY —Donna Clayton
Loving the Boss

Cindy Cooper dreamed of marrying her boss, even though she doubted handsome executive Kyle Prentice would look twice at a plain Jane like her. But when Cindy's true beauty was revealed, could she trust that Kyle's sudden attraction was more than skin-deep?

#1343 A RUGGED RANCHIN' DAD—Kia Cochrane
Fabulous Fathers

Stone Tyler loved his wife and his son, but tragedy had divided his family. Now this rugged rancher would do everything in his power to be the perfect daddy—and recapture his wife's heart—before time ran out....

#1344 MARRY ME, KATE—Judy Christenberry
The Lucky Charm Sisters

He needed to prevent his mother from pushing him up the aisle. She needed money to rebuild her father's dream. So William Hardison and Kate O'Connor struck a bargain. They'd marry for one year, and their problems would be solved. It was the perfect marriage—until a little thing called love complicated the deal....

#1345 GRANTED: A FAMILY FOR BABY—Carol Grace
Best-Kept Wishes

All Suzy Fenton wanted was a daddy for her sweet son. But sexy sheriff Brady Wilson thought his able secretary was looking for Mr. Right in all the wrong places. And that maybe, just maybe, her future husband was right before her eyes....

#1346 THE MILLION-DOLLAR COWBOY—Martha Shields
Cowboys to the Rescue

She didn't like cowboys, but rodeo champion Travis Eden made Becca Lawson's pulse race. Maybe it was because they had grown up together or because Travis was unlike any cowboy she had ever met. Or maybe it was purely a matter of the heart....

#1347 FAMILY BY THE BUNCH—Amy Frazier
Family Matters

There was never any doubt that rancher Hank Whittaker wanted a family—he just wasn't expecting five children all at once! Or beautiful Nessa Little, who came with them. Could Nessa convince the lone cowboy to take this ready-made family into his heart?